Addison Peale Russell

A Club of One

Passages from the Note-Book of a Man who Might Have Been Sociable

Addison Peale Russell

A Club of One
Passages from the Note-Book of a Man who Might Have Been Sociable

ISBN/EAN: 9783337141073

Printed in Europe, USA, Canada, Australia, Japan

Cover: Foto ©Andreas Hilbeck / pixelio.de

More available books at **www.hansebooks.com**

A Club of One

PASSAGES FROM THE NOTE-BOOK OF
A MAN WHO MIGHT HAVE
BEEN SOCIABLE

WITH MARGINAL SUMMARY

By THE EDITOR

BOSTON AND NEW YORK
HOUGHTON, MIFFLIN AND COMPANY
The Riverside Press, Cambridge
1893

ELEVENTH EDITION.

The Riverside Press, Cambridge, Mass., U. S. A.
Electrotyped and Printed by H. O. Houghton & Company.

EDITOR'S PREFACE

A PRETTY *good-sized drawer, locked and padlocked, was found filled with the manuscripts from which these Passages were taken. I have presumed to give them the title they bear, the author of them having departed this life. It is very evident they were not designed for the public. They were written purely for occupation, there is not a doubt of it. The author, a reader and thinker, though an invalid, could not be idle. He read and he thought, and sometimes he recorded. He has said some things that have not been said before, and has said them in his own way. Except in the earlier pages, almost all that related to his aches and ailments has been omitted, — the editor knowing perfectly well that his many complaints would very soon weary if not disgust the reader, when*

*the purpose constantly in view was to enter-
tain and enlighten him.* **Another** *effect* **has
been to** *keep* **down the** *bulk,* **as** *the fashion*
seems to be going out of *rating* *books* **by** *the*
pound.

CONTENTS

	PAGE
A Birthday Lamentation	9
His Left Ear Now	10
Snowing Again	12
His Hair Trimmed Too Close	13
An Unaccountable Twitching	14
The Duke of Queensberry Plan	15
The Bit of Potato Skin	17
"The Abominable Sparrows"	18
Discharges his Doctor	20
The Apothecary's Bill	21
Blue Glass Experience	23
Too Much Blue Glass	24
The New Doctor	26
It Rains — Studies Dante	29
Continues the Study of Dante	36
Exhaustion — Then and Now	40
The Blinds Left Open	43
Horn-Blowing	43
Marriage of December and May	48
Importance of Taking Care of his Health	51
Hates Disputation	56

Pledge-Making and Pledge-Taking 60

The North East Wind 60

Age and Want 64

Town and Country 68

The Children 75

Is Life Worth Living ? 81

The Stupid Doctors — Old Remedies 82

Diseased Sensibility 86

Politeness 92

Compliments 95

The Lawyers 98

An Honest Man 107

Killing the Devil 113

The Gout Now 116

Counts his Pulsations 117

The Man and the Woman 120

The Professional Invalid 124

The Professional Invalid Continued 130

Foster's Essays — Margaret 136

The Perfect Ballad 140

Saint Valentine's Day 142

" My Books ! " 148

Books ! Books ! 151

The Dance of the Pill Boxes 160

" My Grindstone Library " 164

Ancient and Modern Quakerism 172

Man and Monkey 176

Metaphysics and Political Economy 186

" Lord, Have Mercy " 188

Evil Communications 195

Sin and Bile 199

The Thoroughly Cultivated Man 204

The Business of Reforming 212

Eyes for the Blind 219

The Burden and the Mystery 225

A Fogy, and Not a Reformer 235

Another President Elected 240

Dimensions of Hell 240

The Human Brain 241

"My Wife" 249

A CLUB OF ONE

O H, the burden of my life! Why A birthday lamentation. am I spared to see another birthday? Poor miserable me! an aggregation of miseries. I live to suffer, and suffer to live. I have used drugs enough to poison all the fishes in all the oceans. Doctors many and doctors different have visited me, times innumerable; but to how little purpose! According to the Zendavesta, the number of diseases wrought by the witchcraft of the evil one was "nine, and 99,999 diseases. ninety, and nine hundred, and nine thousand, and nine times ten thousand." Ninety - nine thousand nine hundred and ninety-nine seems to me to be a low estimate. The devil, I believe, has been industriously inventing and introducing new ones ever since the sacred book was written. Considering his genius for mischief, and his hatred of the human race, the arch-enemy must have doubled the number, at least, in the two or three thousand years since Zoroaster. Indeed, when I think of what I have myself endured, I conclude the number incomputable. Everything short of death and absolute insanity I have suffered, in body and in mind. In the thirty years since I began to suffer exclusively (never having seen a well day in all that time), every organ has again and again been attacked, and every function disturbed. I have been the victim, I do believe, of every torture known to mankind. But for the hopes of orthodoxy, I — But I am forgetting the powders the doc- tor left me for the pain in my great toe — one to be taken every two hours, till the pain leaves or decidedly abates. The powder was hardly down when another toe was attacked! Two powders now, I suppose, every two hours. My poor toes!

Worse and worse, after a wretched night. It is my left ear now that is tortured. The acuteness of the pain may be guessed upon reflecting that the nerves of hearing (according to Dr. Holmes) clasp the roots of the brain as a creeping vine clings to the bole of an elm. If I am to live, I want

my two ears, that I may execrate the clock
at every tick, as I lie awake the long nights.
The ear — what a wonderful arrangement
it is! The eyes shut; other organs are
suspended; but the ear is ever open and
attentive, — ready to alarm at any disturb-
ance. That striking and quaint passage in *Passage from Rabelais.*
Rabelais occurs to me: "Nature, I am
persuaded, did not without a cause frame
our ears open, putting thereto no gates at
all, nor shutting them up with any manner
of inclosures, as she hath done upon the
tongue, the eyes, and other such out-jut-
ting parts of the body. The cause, as I
imagine, is, to the end that every day and
every night, and that continually, we may.
be ready to hear, and by a perpetual hearing apt to learn." The mighty, miserable
Nimrod! Thinking of my ear, I think of *Nimrod.*
his miserable end, and I think of somebody suffering beside myself. Enraged
(according to a tradition of the Arabs) at
the destruction of his gods by the prophet
Abraham, he sought to slay him, and waged
war against him. But the prophet prayed
to God, and said, "Deliver me, O God, *Abraham's prayer.*
from this man, who worships stones, and
boasts himself to be the lord of all things;"
and God said to him, "How shall I pun-

ish him ?" And **the prophet** answered,
"To Thee armies are as nothing, and the
strength and power of men likewise. Be-
fore the smallest of thy creatures will they
perish." And God was pleased at the faith

God sent a gnat. of the prophet, **and He** sent a gnat, which
vexed Nimrod day and night, so **that he**
built a room of glass in his palace, that he
might dwell therein and shut out the insect. But the gnat entered also, and passed
by his ear into his brain, upon which it fed,
and increased in size day by day, so that
the servants of Nimrod beat his head with
a hammer continually, **that he** might have
some ease from his pain ; but he died, after

The gnat in Nimrod's brain for 400 years. suffering **these torments for four** hundred
years. **Alas ! (to think** of it) who hath not
his gnat of memory, reflection, or retribu-
tion ?

Snowing again. **Snowing** again ! The great ugly flakes
are covering everything. The air is raw
and chilly. I hate snow. There is noth-
ing interesting about it. It has the ex-
pression of a corpse. It is an obstruction
and a **nuisance. I shall not be** able to take
my accustomed ninety-two paces on the

Chilliness covering his skin like a shroud. veranda to-day on account of it. I feel a
chilliness gradually covering my skin like

a shroud, freezing the millions of pores,
thousands by thousands. The tediousness
of the process, as well as the distress of
it. My poor bones! The marrow of them
now seems to be freezing, too. What am
I to do? It is a question of woolens, per- *A question of woolens.*
haps. I tried white — it is too chilling; I
tried red — it is too irritating. I believe I
shall try pink — a delicate shade. I am
resolved upon pink — the flush of a glow-
ing sun-burn on a tender part. Pink it
shall be. If satisfactory, I shall tell nobody. The precious secret! My poor
brain is not to be worried discovering relief for other people. Let them suffer!
Who cares for me? Brayed in a mortar
may all the world be, for aught that I care.
It vexes me to think that I have nobody to *Nobody to think for him.*
think for me. I believe that if my brain
could rest for a while I should be better.
But the necessity of thinking, thinking
— always of myself. Poor me! Nobody
pities me. The universal selfishness! Ah,
my eyes are ready to burst out with suffering, as they say Swift's did. I can hardly
see the lines I write on. My wife —

My barber, in cutting my hair this morn- *His hair trimmed too close.*
ing, trimmed it too close, and a terrible

cold is the consequence. I feel a conges-
tion traveling up my spine at a dangerous
rate. Parts of me unknown to me till now
are being pulled to pieces pitilessly. The
eider-down cushion presses hard against
my shoulder like the burden of Atlas. The
mischief must be driven out. Water! hot
water! The feet must be boiled. Ah!

Boils his feet. an hour's boiling, and a few chapters of
Job. I feel better.

> " **Smoothed the** pillow, the throbbing brain
> Survives the pang, and sleeps again."

A twitching in one of his calves. Last night **one of my** calves was seized
with an unaccountable twitching. It
seemed a forerunner of something serious.
An infinite piercing followed, like ten thousand needles. **Piercing,** piercing — like
pins piercing a pippin, but with inexpres-
sible pain. It fairly took my breath away
for a time. The doctor was dispatched
for. He came, but not in a very good

The brute of a doctor. humor. The brute has no feeling. I pay
him my dollars and he should feel for my
woes. He listened — not like a man — not
even **professionally** — but like an insensible machine. **My blood boiled** like Ætna.
I had no weapon to strike him **with.** I
could see that he questioned the descrip-

tion I gave him of my sufferings. This
morning I was better, thank the Lord!
The stinging, penetrating pains had left
me; but no thanks to the monster's dis-
gusting remedy. I did n't take his miser- *Did n't take his bolus.*
able bolus — big enough for an elephant.

An idea! The old Duke of Queens- *The Duke of Queensberry and Chinese plan.*
berry paid his physicians on the plan
adopted by the Chinese emperors, — so
much per week for keeping him alive. Excellent! with the privilege of discharging
them at any time for offensiveness or in-
humanity. The creatures like money, and,
employed on that principle, they would be
more apt to be faithful, encouraging, and
sympathizing. I have known so many of
them, in my long career of distress, — of
every grade and of every school, — from
the Sangrado type, with his thunder and
lightning, to the latest disciple of Hahnemann, with his infinitesimals and attenuated
moonshine, that, as a necessary evil, I feel
myself as competent as any one to judge
of them. Capital! I think I shall try *Concludes to try it.*
the Chinese and Queensberry plan. My
wife — But an instance in point before I
forget it (which deserves to be set down),
illustrating the profession — almost without

an exception. **They are a** lying, mercenary **set.** An intelligent friend **of mine,** broken seriously in health by the agitations **and** successes of **the** civil war-time, quitted his comfortable **home** and large business, **and** went abroad **for** treatment by **an eminent** Paris physician. He did not improve, **after** many visits and prescriptions ; and the great doctor, perceiving that his patient's **patience was** failing, recommended him **very kindly to another great** doctor in Berlin. **My poor invalid friend,** before presenting **the letter of introduction** he bore **with** him, **not a little shaken** in his confidence after the long, unsuccessful treatment, **had the curiosity and good sense to** break the seal and read **the** message. **It was in good French** (laconic enough), **and to** this effect : **"Paris, Sept. 8, 187-. My** dear Doctor : This will introduce to **you** Mr. K——, of Cincinnati, United States of America. Plenty of money. Nothing the matter with him. Rejoicing to send you **another fat** patient, I remain yours, fraternally. **J. X——." Rascal** and hypocrite ! Jonadab and **Tartuffe combined.** The letter was delivered, **but** only as **a basis for** some good, eloquent, native - American swearing. My friend, after lingering a few

The Paris physician.

Another great doctor in Berlin.

Jonadab and Tartuffe combined.

weeks at Nice and Wiesbaden, returned home, and soon recovered from his dangerous illness, but without the aid of any more distinguished doctors.

At breakfast this morning I inadvertently swallowed a bit of the skin of a baked potato, about the size of a shirt button. It was hard and chippy, and hurt as it went. Its edge must have teeth, like a circular saw. I feel it sawing its way, through the thirty feet of passage, and the fear is that it may lodge in the cæcum. The idea is horrible, and hurts my poor brain as the potato skin does my imperiled stomach. It cannot be that a man in my disordered state, with such an infinity of awful experiences, could have been inattentive or careless in so important a matter as eating. But I must take to inspecting dangerous articles of food with a handglass, and arrange for a stronger light to eat by. Two or three ugly obstructing fruit trees must be cut down. Oh! Ah! Horrors! The remorseless potato skin is ripping its way. Why does n't the doctor come? Lingering, I suppose, stupidly, at the bedside of somebody that is dying, to the neglect of his patient who always pays him, and

Swallows a bit of potato skin.

Its teeth like a circular saw.

Determines to inspect dangerous articles of food.

whose existence is of **such** importance to himself. **But, he** comes — the laggard!

The doctor heartless. **Heartless** again! **He does not** seem to be so **much alarmed** as myself at my situation. **He counsels relaxing** remedies, and quiet. A **very** slight **change** of position, **I feel,**

The only hope. might be fatal. **The** only hope is in the absolute expulsion of the dangerous substance — my poor stomach being too weak **to be** counted on as an auxiliary. The **doctor is well-read in his profession,** and **says there is no case of the sort** mentioned **in the books; but the gravity of my condition** does **not seem to be** appreciated by him. Anxiety about it ought to whiten **his hair.** Than the **fanged edge of a bit** of potato skin, there could be nothing more appall**ing.** The slightest movement, and I

A pang that is awful. feel a pang that is awful. The doctor, **I** think, only feigns alarm; but tries to sympathize, — which is something unusual. His other sick and dying patients must be cared **for by** his youthful copartner and **nurses: all the resources of** his wisdom and **experience must** be expended on me.

The abominable English sparrows. It was the design that **I** should sleep late this morning, but the abominable English sparrows waked me long before daylight.

Their multitudinous chatter was not only disturbing — it was malicious ; as there can be no doubt of their happiness over my miseries. They peeped impishly through every space in the blinds big enough to admit a sunbeam. There was something Mephistophelean in their mocking irony. Cursèd be the man — the enemy of the peace of all civilized Americans — who imported them. He should be incinerated, and his ashes blown by the four winds to the four quarters of the globe. The detestable little pests should be exterminated by all means. . They have no friends but enthusiastic farmers and gardeners, who insist that they live mainly on worms and insects. And they stubbornly refuse to admit that they drive away other birds ! As to that, however, I do not care ; as, in my present humor, the destruction of all birds would be pleasant enough to me. Love for them, so flippantly expressed, is only, I believe, an affectation. I would offer a generous premium for the heads of every hundred sparrows ; or, what might be better and more effective, a very large sum to the leader and authority in ladies' hats in Paris to make them fashionable, as an adornment, for a single season. By

A curse upon the man who imported them.

Love for them an affectation.

whatever means, it is of the utmost importance that they should be gotten rid of.

*Dirty little
things.*

They are dirty little things. It is necessary for very well-dressed people to adopt every precaution to protect themselves against them. Only yesterday a precious decoction — mellowing in the sun — to be used as a lotion on certain parts of my poor body — was incautiously left un-

*A single
sparrow
spoiled the
whole pot.*

covered, and a single sparrow defiled the whole pot. They are too dirty to eat, or they would long since have been consumed by the hungry.

*Discharges
the doctor.*

Another crisis. I have been obliged to discharge my doctor. The fellow was more and more offensive to me, and finally became unendurable. So I sent for him this morning to dismiss him. The Satanic grin on his face when he came in was something exasperating. His utter want of sympathy, and growing tendency to say disagreeable and impertinent things, prepared me to be rude to him; but I repressed myself in good taste, and begged him to sit down. It is a wonder the necessities of the creature had not made him humble, or at least considerate. How a man as poor as he is can be insolent to

those who feed him is past my comprehension. He had drawn and drawn upon
me, till the balance I owed him was trifling.
Ever since I asked him to spend a night
with me — a night of unexampled torture
— and sleep on the comfortable sofa, so
long the bed of my poor departed dog —
he has shown a very ugly disposition to- *Showed an ugly disposi-*
wards me, in spite of his effort to conceal *tion.*
it. His ridiculous pride, I suppose, was *His ridicu-*
piqued by the proposition ; but what busi- *lous pride.*
ness has a poor devil of a doctor with
pride, I should like to know. Pride is a
luxury appropriate to the opulent. And
the smell of tobacco always in his clothing was as offensive to me as his cursèd
haughtiness. Some outdoor air had to be
let in after his visits to dissipate the
poison, which as often endangered my existence. The disgust of my olfactories at
tobacco is serious enough, but the rude
shock of the freezing air off the snow-
covered earth is deadly. The relief that I *Relief in be-*
feel in being rid of the miserable creature *ing rid of him.*
might be considered a feeble counterfeit of
pleasure, if such a visitation were not impossible to an enduring sufferer like me.

The regular vexation. The quarterly

The quarterly bill of the apothecary. bill of the apothecary is just in. A man of less experience in such things would be driven to madness by them. The many items, and the swindling aggregate! It would not do to question the rascality, as being robbed is preferable to being gossiped about by the robber. I very well *Compact of villainy.* understand the compact of villainy existing between the druggists and the doctors. The profits on the detestable drugs are so enormous that the druggist can well afford to pay the doctor an enormous per cent. on his prescriptions. I have heard incredible stories of their petty partnership meannesses, which have been more than confirmed by my own unfortunate experience. An article not worth a dime is charged a dollar for. A Latin name for a nothing makes it something, and dignifies the swindle. No wonder the apothecary rides in his carriage, and impecunious doctors, like the one I have just discharged, *Pocketfuls of Habanas.* carry pocketfuls of Habanas. The latter have only to supply themselves, at convenience, from the cases of the generous druggists who compound their prescriptions. The thing has been (or something like it) from Hippocrates, and will be, till the crack of doom. A check for it only

settles the bill for the quarter, — it does
not check the villainy, but encourages it.
It seems, indeed, unpleasantly like com-
pounding it. But I am a poor reformer.
I hate reformers.

This morning I had the plain glass re- *Blue glass*
moved from the south windows and the
blue glass put in : the sash-frames containing it, I mean. Temporary only, of course,
as the influence of the blue light is too
stimulating to me to be risked long at a *Care to be*
time. I have tried it thoroughly, and be- *exercised.*
come convinced of its singular efficacy.
Pleasonton, perhaps, claims too much for
it, but blue glass, none the less, is a bene-
faction. Some of my most distressing ailments have been relieved by it. Care, of
course, must be exercised in its use, as excess, I know, would be hurtful. I wonder
its supreme value as a remedial agent has *Its supreme*
value as a
not been more generally acknowledged. *remedial*
agent.
As a stimulant, merely, it is wonderful.
Upon me, as such, its effect is supernatural.
I sit now (not too far from the window)
with the supernal light pouring over me.
It influences me so — is so stimulating —
that I thought a moment ago I could detect something like an impulse of pleasant-

ness in my being. **An** effect like that, —
with nothing of the violent or spasmodic
in it, — I am prepared to say, is next **to**
miraculous. Blessèd be blue glass ! It is

Blessèd be blue glass.

impossible to estimate its value to civilization and **mankind.** Systems of education,
systems of philosophy, of medicine, of religion even, may be upturned by it. We
do not think of the remarkable influence
that color exerts upon the character and
conduct of men. Rösch and Esquirol af-

Influence of color upon character and conduct.

firm that dyers **of scarlet** become choleric
by virtue of occupation **alone.** I am satis-
fied that the extraordinary growth that
man would attain — intellectual and moral,
as well as physical — by judicious **and**
scientific use of blue glass would be marvelous. We can yet only begin to conjecture — much less to know — the universal
benefits to result from the great discovery.

Indulgence, as usual, is followed by evil

Too much blue glass.

effects. **I** spent too many hours in the
blue light, **and** am suffering from the consequences. Four **or five** hours is the utmost that **I have been** accustomed to risk
in it, but yesterday **I** extended the time **to**
six. **The** effect of the excess was alarm-
ing. A flush of exaltation came upon me

like a paroxysm. I hurried on my blue flannel, which, as a precaution, I always use to let myself gently down to normal wretchedness, that nature at last seems to have suited me better to endure than comparative comfort even — to say nothing of happiness. The blue flannel I find very *Efficacy of blue flannel.* safe, following the blue light; they seem indeed, in a manner, to be concurrent remedies. And as a further precaution, after several hours in the blue rays, I sleep for a night or two between blue blankets. *Blue blankets.* They are an invention of my own, and a perfect specific. Though last night my faith in them was a little shaken, as they did not quite prevent the always to be apprehended aches that are almost sure to follow a course of blue glass — aches that my mother used to call, to her complaining children, " growing pains " — sure evidences of the prodigious value of the discovery as an elixir and vivifier. Accompanying the " pains " were visions and *Visions and schemes.* schemes, numerous and varied — such as disturb the heads of youth, and make them anxious to try themselves in the "muddle" of life. It seems a thousand years since I first learned that the former meant growth and the latter hope — anticipating manhood.   I dreamed of the time agone, with a feeling suggestive of something faintly like pleasure : —

> " I flew to the pleasant fields traversed so oft,
>   In life's morning march when my bosom was young;
> I heard my own mountain goats bleating aloft,
>   And knew the sweet strain that the corn-reapers
>   sung " : —

but questioned my identity at the same time.   That a hopeful boy should have *A miserable* become so miserable a man seemed im-
man.
possible — against nature.   Over and over I turned in my bed, a hundred times — re-sisting, as I best could, the aches and pains, and schemes and visions.   The result of it all is, a miserable condition, and I have
Sends for sent for a doctor, — the best that I could
another
doctor. think of in acute and dangerous cases.   I hope, at least, that he is not a donkey and an ignoramus, to torment me as his pred-ecessor did.

Some obser-   I think I can tolerate my new doctor.
vations upon
the new doc- He seems intelligent, with the instincts of
tor.
a gentleman.   The longer we talked the more I perceived his penetration.   As Em-erson said of Goethe, he seemed to see out of every pore of his skin.   His language shows him to be a scholar, and I hope he

has some general knowledge of literature. In that case I need not repress a tendency to literary reference, as he will understand me when I talk. It seems a shame that the hundred worthies on my shelves should be silent — being never referred to, or encouraged to speak. As we conversed, I noticed that his eye ran over them with an expression of intelligence and enthusiasm. I die for fitting companionship. The sordidness of men! How they are wrapped up in themselves and their little interests! A wise doctor should be wise *Requisites to* in everything. He should know men — *wisdom in* all sorts of men. In questions of race he *the profession.* should see behind and before — progenitors and inheritors alike. Philosophies and religions should be familiar to him. Books and their makers should be the objects of his affectionate regard. He should, like Lamb, kiss a volume of Burns with tenderness, and bow with reverence before Shakespeare or Bacon. This man, to some extent, seems to be the possessor of such a sentiment. His intelligence has the reflection of breadth and the look of wisdom. His apparent liberality of judgment seems to be the result of facile intercourse with various minds. The commerce of intellect, it is truly said, loves distant shores. The small retail dealer trades only with his neighbors; when the great merchants trade, they link the four quarters of the globe. In

Four great merchants. Brooklyn, one night, I met four such. They seemed to have been everywhere and to have seen everything. They talked, not of processes, but of results. Every sentence was freighted with wisdom, and was compact enough for a proverb. Their eyes as well as their minds seemed to have a measuring and weighing habit. This man, of course, is not a man of that type. If he were, he would not be a drudging doctor.

Manner of the new physician. His considerate and attentive manner pleases me. It cannot be wholly the result of training. Selfish, no doubt, he is; everybody is that. If he is prompt, submissive, and faithful, I shall try to put up with the objectionable in him as it de-

Head and heart. velops. His head, I believe, is more than an average one; but his heart — of what quality and composition is that? Is there feeling in it? — red blood? — the blood of a man? If when I groan or cry out in a paroxysm of pain the laughing machinery should play about the corners of his mouth, I should feel like killing him. I will not be gibed at by a monkey of a doctor. The

way he dusts his feet and lifts his hat and removes his gloves is in his favor. He is not constantly stroking his beard and clearing his throat in a Sir Oracle way. The per- *The per-fumery he uses.* fumery he uses ; I cannot quite make out what it is. It is not agreeable, and not quite disgusting. I shall have to ask him the ingredients of the stuff. You cannot guess from the smell. A dung-hill at a distance, said Coleridge, sometimes smells like musk, and a dead dog like elder-flowers. He is a believer in blue glass, I am pleased *A believer in blue glass.* to know, and carries his faith to the point of devotion. Blue glass he unqualifiedly pronounces a good thing ; but believes with me that, as with every other good thing, one may have too much of it. My blue woolens, as a gradient, so to speak, or anti- dote for excess, he is in raptures over — especially the blue blankets. He promised me to think profoundly of the general sub- ject of blue woolens, as an auxiliary in the *Blue wool-ens.* blue glass treatment, and make such sug- gestions as to shades of the same as might occur to his scientific judgment.

It rains, and it rains ! The beautiful *It rains.* rain ! The clouds go rolling round, like big black sponges, squeezing themselves out on the chimney **pots.** The gutters run ink. There are people to say it is dreadful. **But** I like **it**; it is in harmony with my feelings. I hate what they call cheerfulness. Irving's description of a rainy day is one of his best productions. It makes dreariness attractive. Happiness, after all, is, I believe, but a bit of acting. Life is not a comedy — it is a tragedy. No life **is** satisfactory. " Youth," says Beaconsfield, "**is a** blunder, manhood **a struggle,** old **age a regret."** **The most** fortunate are disappointed. **Stephen, in the** story, understood it : "'T is a' a muddle." The Japanese **have a proverb that** epitomizes the unsatisfactoriness **of life:** "**If you** hate a man, **let him live."** Their little children, in school, are taught **to** repeat a verse which in **English would run in** this wise : —

Life a disappointment.

" Color and perfume vanish away.
  What can be lasting in this world?
  To-day disappears in the abyss of nothingness;
  It **is** but the passing image of a dream, and **causes** **only a slight** trouble."

Vanity of vanities, saith the preacher; all is **vanity. It is on a day like this that** I particularly like Dante's Inferno **(the** other parts of the Comedy I do not like). Cary's translation, with Doré's illustrations, is delight-

Studies Dante.

ful ; though I do not like the text so well
as John Carlyle's literal rendering.   In the
latter you get at the sense, as in Hayward's translation of Faust.   Scholars, I
think, should translate poetry, not poets.
The Iliad of Pope is confirmation.   Pope's *Bits of crit-icism.*
genius is conspicuous : not quite so much
so as Homer's : Homer you never quite
lose sight of.   Carlyle's Inferno is Dante's ;
you never think of the Scotchman.   And
it is a very Murray's as a guide-book.   I
make free use of it.   There are two of you
with Virgil.   You go at leisure through the
pleasant scenes.   You read the inscription *Inscription over the gate.*
over the gate as you enter : " Through me
is the way into the doleful city ; through
me the way into the eternal pain ; through
me the way among the people lost.   Justice moved my High Maker ; Divine Power
made me, Wisdom Supreme, and Primal
Love.   Before me were no things created,
but eternal I endure.   Leave all hope, ye
that enter."   You cross the river Acheron.
On its shore all that die under the wrath of
God assemble from every country to be
ferried over by Charon.   He makes them
enter his boat by glaring on them with his
burning eyes.   You go into Limbo.   The *Limbo.*
only pain the spirits there suffer is, that

they live in the desire and without the hope of seeing God. You come into the presence of the Infernal Judge. "There Minos sits horrific, and grins; examines the crimes upon the entrance; judges, and sends according as he girds himself. When the ill-born spirit comes before him, it confesses all; and that sin-discerner sees what place in hell is fit for it, and with his tail makes as many circles round himself as the degrees he will have it to descend. Always before him stands a crowd of them. They go each in its turn to judgment; they tell, and hear; and then are whirled down." Sublime dignity! Doré's picture, it strikes me, is not a good one. He makes the tail of the Judge a serpent, and does not conceal the head. An oversight, I should think, of the artist. You go thence into the place appointed for epicures and gluttons, who set their hearts upon the lowest species of sensual gratification. An unvarying, eternal storm of heavy hail, foul water, and snow, pour down upon them. They are lying prostrate on the ground; and the three-headed monster Cerberus keeps barking over them, and rending them. Doré's conception, in one of the heads, is perfect. Hell itself (of the sen-

The infernal judge.

Criticises Doré's picture.

Cerberus.

sual) is in the face. It is besotted, as well as merciless. Thence to the region of the prodigal and the avaricious. Plutus is at *Plutus.* the entrance, with " clucking voice." Virgil speaks to him : " Peace, cursèd wolf ! Consume thyself internally with thy greedy rage." " As sails, swelled by the wind, fall entangled when the mast gives way ; so fell that cruel monster to the ground." Disgusting creature, as he sits crouching out of view. The artist's genius is conspicuous in the figure. The greediness of the eyes is avarice itself. In the next pic- *The prodi-* ture he vividly depicts the prodigal and the *gal and the* avaricious: they are forever rolling great *avaricious.* weights, and forever smiting each other. " To all eternity they shall continue butting one another." Every muscle seems to be breaking. Thence across the broad marsh, in the fifth circle, where ostentation, arrogance, and brutal anger are punished, to the " joyless city " of Dis. We cross a *The joyless* plain, all covered with burning sepulchres. *city of Dis.* Tongues of fiercer flame speak out of them. And so on we go, and on, we three, by the river of blood, past the obscene harpies, to the plain of burning sand, where an eternal shower of fire is falling ; on again to the crimson stream that runs down to the

Geryon.

centre of hell, when a strange and monstrous shape comes swimming up through the dark air. It is Geryon, the uncleanly image of Fraud. "His face was the face of a just man, so mild an aspect had it outwardly; the rest was all a reptile's body." Upon the "haunch of the dreadful animal" we mount, and are conveyed down to the eighth circle. He moves himself with many a sweeping round, and, setting us down, bounds off, "like an arrow from the string."

Flatterers, liars, seducers.

On the way, we see flatterers, "immersed in filth," and panders, and lying seducers, hurrying along — meeting one another — all naked, and scourged by horned demons. We stop not to see the peculators, and assassins, and tyrants, but take a look at the

The wicked hell-bird.

"wicked hell-bird" on the margin of the boiling pitch — glaring, ready to strike.

The hypocrites.

The hypocrites are interesting, as they walk in slow procession, heavy laden with cloaks of lead, which are gilded and of dazzling brilliancy on the outside. A thief, with a load of serpents on his haunch and a fiery dragon on his shoulders, comes shouting along. The shadow of Mahomet, rent asunder from the chin downward, displays the conscious vileness and corruption of his doctrines. From the arch of the tenth

chasm are heard the wailings of falsifiers of
every kind. Thence along the brim of the
Pit, to mighty Antæus, who takes us in his *Antæus.*
arms and sets us down "into the bottom of
all guilt," or lowest part of hell, where
eternal cold freezes and locks up Cocytus,
the marsh that receives all its rivers. Here
is Cain, who killed his brother Abel. Then
to the end—the last circle of Cocytus,
which takes its name (Judecca) from Judas
Iscariot, and gaze in admiration at the
arch-traitor Satan himself, "Emperor of *Satan him-*
the Realm of Sorrow." He too is pursued *self.*
by his own sin. All the streams of guilt *Streams of*
keep flowing back to him, as their source, *ing back.*
and from beneath his three faces (shadows
of his own consciousness) issue forth the
mighty wings with which he struggles, as
it were, to raise himself ; and sends out
winds that freeze him only the more firmly
in his ever swelling marsh. "From Beelze-
bub as far removed as his tomb extends is a
space, not known by sight but by the sound
of a rivulet descending in it, along the hollow of a rock which it has eaten out with
tortuous course and slow declivity." We
enter by that hidden road, to return into *Return to*
the bright world : mounting up through "a *world.*
round opening the beauteous things which

Heaven bears;" **and** thence we issue out, "again to see the stars."

Continues the study of Dante. All **honor to Doré** for his pictures of Antæus! They are tremendous, — **the** mighty conceptions of genius. But he did not attempt the Devil! After his success with the poet, in the frontispiece, I wonder that he hesitated. There is gloom there that is profound. It is not at all strange **that the people should have** pointed at the **man with such a face, and said** to one another as **he passed along, "**There goes the **man who has been in hell." The** Knight **of** The Sorrowful Countenance had a smil-**ing face compared with the poet of** the **damned. Pictures so vivid and** interesting **as these of Doré's it is** an enjoyment to

A Dantesque passage from Heine. study. He should **have** illustrated a pas-sage **in** Heine that is so Dantesque in description. It is of **a** remarkable quarrel in **a** little hospital at Cracow where he was an **accidental spectator,** where **it** was interest-**ing to hear the** sick mocking and revil-**ing each other's infirmities, how** emaciated **consumptives ridiculed those** who **were** bloated with **dropsy, how** one laughed at the cancer **in the nose** of another, and **he** again jeered the locked jaws and distorted eyes of his neighbor, until finally those who were mad with fever sprang naked from bed, and tore the coverings and sheets from the maimed bodies around, and there was nothing to be seen but misery and mutilation. Strange! that the literary outlaw who describes to us so faithfully the scene should have had a face full of all tenderness — as youthful and beautiful as Keats' or Hunt's. And so I go on, on — curiously and reflectingly — lingering over the matchless achievement of the poet and the illustrations of the artist. I contemplate the miserable, and participate in their wretchedness. In an access of abnormal misery, such as comes to me often in these later days of unendurable existence, I feel myself hardly less wretched than the miserable I have been contemplating. Hence the interest I cannot help expressing. It is but community of feeling. Proverbially, misery loves company. Goldsmith expressed the necessity in a letter to Bob Bryanton, though the gentle Goldsmith's misery, I imagine, must have been more a matter of fancy than of reality. "You," said he, "seem placed at the centre of fortune's wheel, and, let it revolve ever so fast, are insensible to the motion.

Face of the literary outlaw.

Abnormal misery.

Goldsmith

I seem to have been tied to the circumference, and whirled disagreeably around as if on a whirligig." To another, about the same time, he wrote, " I have been for some years struggling with a wretched being. What has a jail that is formidable ? I shall at least have the society of wretches, and such is to me true society." The

Wailings of the damned. wailings of the damned take the tone of my own sufferings. Their miseries are real, and not fanciful. They are fated, too, and sympathy expended upon them is wasted. Their pains are penalties ; mine, I feel, are vengeful and causeless. Enough perdition here, certainly, for me. Paradise only could compensate. An infinity of delight must balance a life-time of anguish. The damned, consequently, I can hear howl and rage without being distressed. Justice doomed them, and the divine wrath is un-

Hell a necessity. quenchable and immutable. Hell is a necessity. As I go through, with Dante, I find places for my enemies. Those who take pains so far to conceal and qualify their obduracy and selfishness as to now and then make a show of sympathy for me, I can imagine in the presence of the Infernal Judge, confessing themselves, and being whirled down, according as the coils

of the remorseless tail determine, to suffer
and writhe with the multitude of their
fellows, ever and ever, without hope. And
here I cannot help remarking upon something very interesting in the poet. Time
and again he seems touched by the wretchedness he encounters, and gives unmistak-
able sign of sympathy. As in the case of
meeting the impulsive and surprised lovers, Francesca and Paolo : he fell to the
ground as if dead, when he heard their
painful story : though the manifestation
may have been to a degree selfish, as the
sigh of Francesca — " There is no greater
pain than to recall a happy time in wretchedness " — must have reminded him of his
sainted Beatrice. "I fainted," he says,
" with pity, as if I had been dying ; and
fell, as a dead body falls." The weakness
was natural in view of the painful remembrance. All in all, I think the historian
and poet of hell would have been com-
panionable to me. He could have understood my distresses, and entered deeply
into the bottomless abysses of my anguish.
When I groaned, his wisdom would pene-
trate the cause. When I writhed, his observations of the damned would diagnose
the paroxysm. When the universal pain

Something very interesting in the poet.

Beatrice.

The poet of hell as a companion.

prostrated me, as Pascal was prostrated, hopelessly, his quick sense of misery could conjecture the incalculable endurance. But I must live on, I suppose, to the end, without intelligent and proper sympathy. The common mind and common heart are incapable of it. It would require a genius of observation in misery and the heart of a celestial to properly sympathize with me.

Exhausted by writing. The time I spent at my desk day before yesterday and the day before that about exhausted me. Time was when I could write and write, without limit. The words ran away from my pen with the flowing ink. At a time, too, when I had nothing to say. I had not learned to unlearn what I had learned, and knew nothing. We gather and throw away as we ascend and descend the hill of life (wisdom I will not *The little child.* call it). Once I saw a little child, in swaddling clothes, on the floor. Some one gave it a big red marble (too big to put into its mouth), which it took in one hand ; then another marble was given to it, which it took with the other. Hardly had the little thing time to realize its possessions, when a bright golden one appeared to vex it. There were three marbles, now, and it had but two hands. Another and another and another was presented to it. What was it to do? It dropped and seized and *Wearied by its efforts.* seized and dropped, till, exhausted by its efforts, it fell asleep — the coveted marbles rolling away — not one of them all remaining in its possession. So it is with all, — at the top and at the bottom of the hill of life : empty - handed as the little child — the same at the end as at the beginning. Now, when I have something to say, I have not the strength to say it. Literary schemes dreamed out, all had to be abandoned. I had at one time something very compendious in contemplation. Years of effort would have been necessary to achieve it. Long ago I destroyed all vestiges of preparation. Note-books and note-books went *Note-books destroyed.* into the fire, and a large part of my cherished hopes went with them. They were so much of myself. The batteries of the brain — how many! — had been operated to produce them. The brain! The minuteness of its parts and the magnitude of its achievements! A billion of the starry brain-cells, says Holmes, could be packed in a cubic inch, and the convolutions contain one hundred and thirty - four cubic inches! Going too long, the great scheme aborted.   The loss of the half-formed thing left a void that has **never** been filled. Empty seemed everything for a space, and the ruin it made has many a time reminded me of **the** lady on the point of marriage, whose intended husband usually traveled by the stage-coach to visit her.   She went one day to meet him, and found instead of him an old friend who came to announce **to her** the tidings of his sudden death. She uttered a scream, and piteously exclaimed, " He is dead ! "   But then all consciousness **of the** affliction that had befallen her ceased.   " From that fatal moment," says the **recorder of the** incident, " this unfortunate **female daily** for fifty years, in all seasons, traversed the distance **of a** few miles to the spot where she expected her future husband to alight from the coach ; and every day she uttered in a plaintive tone, 'He is not come yet !   I will return to-morrow ! ' "   My poor wasted **preparatory** effort is dead, buried, — I wish it could be forgotten.   A record of the solemn **entombment is** inscribed in all the waste **places** remaining.   And here I am writing about the **figment,** when I ought to **be in bed between my** blue blankets. My wife —-

*The great
scheme
aborted.*

*" He is
dead ! "*

*The solemn
entombment.*

Incautiously a section of the blinds was *The blinds left open.*
left open, and the blazing sun waked me
long before my accustomed time to rise.
" Sun ! how I hate thy beams ! " once exclaimed Dr. Johnson, — I imagine under
similar circumstances. I quoted the lexi-
cographer with emphasis. The sun ! — it
makes everything too visible ; and the
Doctor, with his enthusiasm of sadness, and
observation, which, " with extensive view,"
had surveyed " mankind from China to
Peru," was moved by disquieting disclos-
ures. In the shadows only, and through *Observation and intro-*
smoked glass, as it were, men of the type *spection.*
of the Doctor should scan themselves and
their fellow mortals. Too much light is ex-
posing, as a slab of wood turned over on a
bright sunshiny day in June reveals a multitude of hideous creatures, of manifold
kinds, which scamper and crawl away in
terror at the sun's all-seeing rays.

I am vexed to madness. A fellow with *Infuriated by a horn-*
a horn in a top room of a tall building in *blower.*
the neighborhood was tugging and tugging
away for hours last night at a few notes of
detestable " Shoo Fly," to the annoyance
or horror of every one who heard, over and
over, ever and ever, the same miserable

few **notes.** The **rascal,** blowing so hard
and exhaustingly, **had to** have air in abun-

dance, so his two windows were wide open,
and the diabolical sounds produced by **his**
instrument had free exit and opportunity
for torture without stint. It is a wonder
that Dante, **in** all the regions of the
damned, found no place for horn-blowers.

" Hell - fire, kept within proper bounds,"
Fuseli said to Rogers, " is **no** bad thing."
Limbo might do, if the fellows attempted
only the tolerable ; but they keep blow-
ing away forever at what they themselves
and everybody must hate. A vile tune
runs **round the world, and is** the universal
fashion. **Hated, too, all the time it is
being played, or sung. Strange** to think of

— **everybody** hates whistling, and everybody whistles. **It is the thing that** police-
men should be specially instructed to knock
men down **for** doing. " Shoo Fly " in
fashion, you climb to **the** top of Popocate-
petl **and you will** find **a** man there whistling it. As, in riding up town in the evening, **you see an article of dress** adorning
the persons of thousands which struck you
as a novelty **when you rode down in the**
morning. Strange, **how** imitative men are
— monkeys are **not** more so. And the uni-

versal selfishness! The horn-blowers and
the piano-players never think of how they
are vexing nearly all who hear them. Now
and then, only, an interested person is
found to say it is agreeable. In some
houses there is an instrument of torture — *Instruments of torture.*
stringed, springed, padded, or bored — in
every room, which must be endured, — as
the very people would punish you for complaining of it who complain themselves.
The sensitive lady with the sensitive sick
child, whose nerves are torn to pieces by
the squeaking "organ" of a neighbor,
would be furious if her young lady daughter's practicing on the piano by the hour
were complained of in the least degree.
But that aggregation of discords and hor- *A brass-band.*
rors — a brass - band — who can compass
it? who invented it? A friend of mine
was at the Boston Jubilee the other day,
where there were twelve thousand musi-
cians, and he said he had time and again
heard a village brass - band of a dozen
pieces make more noise than the whole
twelve thousand. But, to think of it, nearly
every one, at some time in life, has blown
a horn, or made a noise on an instrument of some sort, to the torment, to a
greater or less extent, of every other man

who heard him, and he should submit to endure like inflictions of others without murmuring. Horns, too, have played so great a part in the history of this world, that perhaps one should not quite lose all consideration for them. Their effect on the wall of Jericho is memorably recorded in Holy Writ. Sometimes I have wondered that the walls of buildings in which brass-bands were playing did not tumble down in the same manner. At Roncesvalles, Orlando, in despair, blew so terrible a blast, that he rent his horn and the veins and sinews of his neck; and Charles, who heard it eight miles off, was hindered by the traitor Ganellon from coming to his assistance. The sound of Nimrod's horn, which Dante heard, on his way, with Virgil, to the lowest part of hell, was louder still. "I heard," says the poet, "a high horn sound so loudly that it would have made any thunder weak." The voice of Fingal, in Ossian, was hardly less loud and terrible than the horns of Orlando and Nimrod. When he raised his voice, "Cromla answered around, the sons of the desert stood still, and the fishes of the troubled sea moved to the depths." At the very times when you most dislike to

Memorable horns.

At Jericho.

At Roncesvalles.

Nimrod's horn.

Fingal's voice.

hear what they call music, your ears are
most open and sensitive to it, and nothing
will shut it out. I have heard a music-
box — set agoing by some sleepless old
bachelor — through a dozen brick walls.
I have heard a hand-organ playing a mile
away. I have heard a girl singing — *A girl's singing.*
screaming, screeching, squalling — when
my ears were bound up and smothered
with pillows. Fortunately, the barbaric
taste generally disappears at manhood, or
the world would be a pandemonium, and
filled with imbeciles and incapables. The
taste for music once become a chronic appe-
tite or passion, all hope of practicalness or
intelligent application in other fields may
be abandoned. Patrick Henry played the *Patrick Henry.*
fiddle — and he played it well, they say
— but he was a great orator — the greatest
perhaps that America has produced. God
Almightly works inscrutably, his wonders
to perform. He doth the incredible and
exceedeth the unimaginable, for his own
wise purposes. Exceptions he creates or *Exceptions.*
permits for encouragement or example.
The old English divine said of strawber-
ries, " Doubtless God could have made a
better berry, but doubtless God never did."
Doubtless God could have permitted a

greater nuisance than attempts at music, but doubtless God never has.

I have just received a complimentary invitation to a wedding. The bridegroom was a man when I was a boy. He must be a good deal past seventy now. The bride, I hear, is not much above twenty. These *Incongruous marriages.* incongruous marriages! The disparity is suggestive. Softening is almost a certain consequence. Young women do not know what they do when they marry old men. Possibly their hope is in the conclusion of the song — that the old brass their old husbands leave them will buy them *Wycherly.* new pans. Old Wycherly was wise in the matter, and the promise he exacted from his young wife is a travesty upon it, in the comedian's best vein. I do not like to think of it; I fear the bursting of a vessel. The old actor, dramatist, and manager, married a girl of eighteen when he was verging on eighty. Shortly after, Providence was pleased, in its mercy to the young woman, to call the old man to another and a better world. But ere he took his final departure from this, he summoned his young wife to his bedside, and *Dying.* announced to her that he was dying; whereupon she wept bitterly. Wycherly lifted himself up in the bed, and gazing with tender emotions on his young, weeping wife, said, "My dearest love, I have a solemn promise to exact from you before I quit you forever here below. Will you assure me my wishes will be attended to by you, however great the sacrifice you may be called on to make?" Horrid ideas of Suttees, of poor Indian widows being called on to expire on funeral pyres, with the bodies of their deceased lords and masters, flashed across the brain of the poor woman. With a convulsive effort and desperate resolution, old Wycherly's young wife gasped out an assurance that his commands, however dreadful they might be, should be obeyed. Then Wycherly, with a ghastly smile, said in a low and solemn voice, "My beloved wife, the parting request I have to make of you is — that when I am gone — (here the young woman sobbed and cried most vehemently) — when I am in my cold grave — (Mrs. Wycherly tore her hair) — when I am laid low — (the disconsolate wife shrieked with grief) — when I am no longer a heavy burden and a tie on you — ("Oh! for Heaven's sake!" exclaimed Mrs. Wycherly, "what am I to do?") — I com-

Exacts a promise from his young wife.

Assures her obedience.

Distress of the poor woman.

mand you, my dear young wife — (said the old, dying comedian) — on pain of incurring my malediction, never to — marry — an old man again!" Mrs. Wycherly dried her eyes, and, in the most fervent manner, promised that she never would; and that faithful woman kept her word for life. There is not much to be said of incongruous marriages after that. It tells the story. Nothing further could be added to it without quoting the lines of Waller, On One Married to an Old Man, which I would rather not repeat. The whole thing is distasteful. An old man — shriveled and shaky — with a pretty young woman on his shrunken arm — is a picture for a satyr to grin at, and a philosopher to deplore. To be pleased with it would require a perverted taste — suggesting the delight of the surgeon, inspecting the blooming cancer, ripe for his pitiless knife. A poor young plant is the virgin green, that feeds on ruins old. Of right poor food are her meals I ween, in his cell so lone and cold. The incompatibility! Only the amalgam of mammon could unite such opposites. It is Plutus's best work, — at which he swells himself to his greatest proportions — jingling his metallic voice ("clucking voice,"

Lines of Waller.

Perverted taste.

Dante calls it), and licking his chaps like a disgusting great boar. Once I attended a wedding of December and May. The tailor had padded the garments of the bride-groom, and the jeweler had hung his diamonds on the bride. The smile of senility brightened the countenance of the one with a stagy light, while all the blood of the heart of the other seemed to be concentrated in her shame-stricken face. What wonder that Hymen blushed, that satyrs grinned, that Virtue felt herself outraged and Religion insulted, when Sin, in priestly robe, with priestly unction, in awful irony, pronounced the accursèd blessing? The occasion was a Vanity Fair indeed, at which a Death's head on a Venus figure was everywhere present; — at the banquet sitting; peering over the shoulders of beauty; drinking its drink from the goblet of Satan; — the latter an invisible and unexpected guest, but the happiest, by all odds, of the party. I went home a sadder man, — with the distressing certainty, that such scenes must continue to be acted before high Heaven, and increase, with the growth of what all men call civilization.

For two or three days I have suffered

December and May.

Awful irony.

Satan an invisible guest.

Suffers supremely.

supremely, and the utmost I could do was
to take care of myself. So long a sufferer,
I have learned to do that. I should have
been dead long ago if I had trusted other
people to look after me. Some very important matter they would have regarded as
a very little thing, and I should be no more.
So, long since, I perceived the importance
of attentive, perpetual observation and care

A little book of duties. of myself. I have a little book of duties,
which I have religiously kept for years, in
which is set down mathematically every
little and great thing pertaining to my
health — when to do certain things, to the
minute, and when to avoid them altogether;
by which means, and by reason of special
sagacity and acumen in all things in which
I myself am interested, I have become a

A genius in care-taking. very genius in self-observation and care-
taking. (Coddling, the brute of a doctor I
lately discharged called it, on one of his last
visits.) But, with all my care, I sometimes
forget a duty, and suffer in consequence.
When I had concluded my last bit of desk-
work, the time had arrived for my ninety-
two paces on the veranda. To my horror,
and, I fear, my everlasting injury, I took
ninety-eight ! And, not observing the tem-
perature as I should (fifteen degrees above

freezing), I wore my light-weight muffler, and my heavy gloves, without lining. The effect of the excess in exercise, and neglect *Effect of excess.* in not sufficiently protecting myself against the severe cold, very soon announced itself in a cough, the most distressing I have had for years. The doctor, however, was prompt, with heroic remedies, and I am better again, thank the Lord! The man seems to know his business, and me, especially. Though he did miscalculate, when he asked me my age! Impertinence! I did n't have the patience or self-possession of About's Greek servant, who, when asked *About's servant.* his age, answered, imperturbably, " My mother wrote it on a piece of paper, and the wind blew it away." Better for doctor and patient if both had had the tact and kindness displayed under not dissimilar circumstances by two eminent English people. Horace Walpole, dining (it is stated) *Walpole and the duchess.* with the Duchess of Queensberry on her birthday (when she had just finished her eightieth year), soon after the cloth was removed, very politely drank her health in a bumper, and added, " May you live, my Lady Duchess, till you begin to grow ugly!" "I thank you, Mr. Walpole," replied her Grace; " and may you long continue your taste for antiquities!" Ah! age and ugliness! "I remember," says the mother of Fanny Kemble, "the dreadful impression made upon me by a story Sir Thomas Lawrence told my mother of Lady J——, (George the Fourth's Lady J——,) who, standing before her drawing-room looking-glass, and unaware that he was in the rooms, exclaimed: 'I swear it would be better to go to hell at once than to live to grow old and ugly.'" Some one asked Fontenelle how old he was. He parried the impertinence delicately: "Hush! Pray don't speak so loud; death seems to have forgotten me, and you may perhaps put him in mind of me." When I get decidedly better, and the conditions are favorable, I mean to express myself at length of this detestable practice. Meantime, discretion! To live to do so important a thing I must look to living. Living! Could some one teach the art! We should all flock to him to learn. Other people we are very wise about. Of ourselves we are ignorant enough. We are constructed to see outwardly, says old Montaigne. Other people's sins trouble us. But here I am, running on. Philosophy to the moon! What care I for it or anything in comparison with

(margin notes:)
Age and ugliness.
Fontenelle.
Living.
Other people's sins.

myself. It is when I forget myself that I suffer most. The consequences of even a moment's abstraction have sometimes been nearly fatal to me. Dreaming one day over some choice sweet amid the treasures of my library, I mistook the tiger on my rug for the veritable beast from Bengal, and started, in a manner to upset all my *His nerves upset.* nerves. Yet

> " Blessèd are the Books, I say,
> For honey of the soul are they."

And I will enjoy them, and dream over them, to the end. Any deprivation before that. The doctor, by the by, promises me an evening of social converse in my library soon. We shall enjoy it together, I think. He has the stuff of a thinker in him : I hope he has good taste. If he should betray a liking for the modern society novel *The modern society novel.* — written to be read without reflection — as a procession or masquerade is viewed, in which one has the slightest interest — I could not help losing respect for him. I do not expect the man to be a Solomon in wisdom, an Emerson in taste, or an angel in virtue. I should be unfit for him if he were. As to angels, they are fancies. Leigh Hunt's conception is the very best, *Hunt's idea of an angel.* I think, that literature has produced. An

angel (he says) is the chorister of heaven,
the page of martyrdom, the messenger from
the home of mothers. He comes to the
tears of the patient, and is in the blush of
a noble anger. He kisses the hand that
gives an alms. He talks to parents of their
departed children, and smooths the pillow of sickness, and supports the cheek of
the prisoner against the wall, and is the
knowledge and comfort which a heart has
of itself when nobody else knows it, and is
the playfellow of hope, and the lark of as-
piration, and the lily in the dusk of adver-

Twisted into contortions. sity. After such a passage, to be twisted
into contortions by a toe-ache is to suffer
a pang of memory and a discouragement
to hope unknown outside the nethermost
abyss of the doomed. A twinge of the
gout, I suspect.

Hates dispu- tation. I hate disputation. My wife — It is not
discussion. It is next thing to scolding.
Gentlemen ought to be able to talk without
disputing ; though no gentleman will introduce into conversation a subject upon which
gentlemen might differ with feeling. That
is the test. A very good man, as the world
goes, sometimes comes in to sit with me
an evening. The politenesses have hardly

been exchanged, when he asks my view of *Bad manners.* something. The view he at once takes to be a deliberate opinion, and falls to combating it, by giving me his opinion of it, to the contrary. As if I cared particularly what he thought about it ! He is too good a man to cultivate tempestuousness. It has been said wisely that no dispute is managed without passion, and yet there is scarce a dispute worth a passion. Anthony *Trollope.* Trollope is said to have been very fond of disputation for its own sake, and once at dinner to have roared out to some one at the end of the table, " I totally disagree with you. What was it you said ? " Fen- *Cooper's story.* imore Cooper related to Moore an anecdote of a disputative man. " Why, it is as plain as that two and two make four." " But I deny that too ; for 2 and 2 make twenty-two." On one occasion when they were together, Dr. Campbell said some- *Dr. Campbell and Dr. Johnson.* thing, and Dr. Johnson began to dispute it. " Come," said Campbell, " we do not want to get the better of one another ; we want to increase each other's ideas." When the erudite Casaubon visited the Sorbonne *Casaubon.* they showed him the hall in which, as they proudly told him, disputations had been held for four hundred years. " And what," said he, "have they decided?" It is expected by nearly every one that everybody will take a side of everything presented, and at the same time show very marked feelings of partisanship — to the point, even, of belligerence. On first nights, in *In the time of Voltaire.* the time of Voltaire, when play-goers were unusually excited, each spectator was asked, as he entered the parquette, "Do you come to hiss?" "Yes." "Then sit over there." But if he answered, "I come to applaud," he was directed to the other side. Thus the antagonistic bodies were massed for action. So, in society, every man is expected to range himself on one side or the other of every subject. Whatever the insufficiency of information and light, he must decide the question, and all questions, at once, that may be presented to him. Alas! to reflection nothing could be more *Montesquieu.* ridiculous. Montesquieu, in one of the Persian Letters, says: "The other day I was at a gathering where I saw a very amusing man. In a quarter of an hour he decided three questions in morals, four historical problems, and five points in physics. I have never seen such a universal decider." Unreasonable and intemperate partisanship prevents intelligent agree.

ment. Lord Burleigh, we are told, was *Lord Bur-leigh.*
once very much pressed by some of the
divines of his time, who waited on him in a
body, to make some alterations in the Lit-
urgy. He desired them to go into the next
room by themselves, and bring him in
their unanimous opinion upon some of the
disputed points. They returned, however,
to him very soon, without being able to
agree. " Why, gentlemen," said he, " how
can you expect that I should alter any
point in dispute, when you, who must be
more competent, from your situation, to
judge than I can possibly be, cannot agree *Doctors dis-agree.*
among yourselves in what manner you
would have me alter it." Benjamin Lay, a
violent reformer and enthusiast, was contemporary with Dr. Franklin, who sometimes visited him. Among other schemes
of reform he entertained the idea of con- *As to con-verting all mankind.*
verting all mankind to Christianity. This
was to be done by three persons — himself
and two other enthusiasts, assisted by Dr.
Franklin. But on their first meeting at
the doctor's house, the three " chosen vessels " got into a violent dispute on points
of doctrine, and separated in ill-humor.
The philosopher, who had been an amused
listener, advised the three sages to give up

the project of converting the world until they had learned to tolerate one another. It was Froude, I believe, who sometimes in impatient moments wished that the laity *Disputatious divines.* would treat their disputatious divines as two gentlemen once treated their seconds, when they found themselves forced into a duel without knowing what they were quarreling about. As the principals were being led up to their places, one of them whispered to the other, "If you will shoot your second, I will shoot mine."

A man called to ask me to sign the Total Abstinence Pledge. He seemed to be a man of sense. I begged him to stay till I prepared a little pledge for him to sign. *Pledge-making and pledge-taking.* He went away. As if pledge-making and pledge-taking were not for two! As if any one existed who could not be embarrassed by a pledge of some sort. As if any man on earth could subscribe to the Ten Commandments and the Sermon on the Mount without reservation or qualification. As if —

The north-east wind. The wind is from the northeast. I felt it approaching very sensibly, long before it came, and prepared for it as I could. I

put on my pink shirt over a chamois jacket.
I poured some Number Six into my boots.
I breakfasted appropriately. I looked to
the window stripping, and double-sashed the
windows. Forewarned, forearmed. When
it came I was ready for it. Mad to be *Mad to be barred out.*
barred out, it went skirring round and
round for a hole to get in at. It dashed
down the flue, filling the room with poisonous gases and smoke. It appeared where
least expected, and where nothing would
keep it out. Ah, the northeast wind ! —
the universal dread. Once hear a Britisher
assail it ! Boreas is a ruffian and a bully,
but the northeast is a rascal. Æolus has *A rascal.*
not such a vicious, ill-conditioned blast in
his puffy bags. It withers like an evil eye ;
it blights like a parent's curse ; is less kind
than ingratitude ; more biting than forgotten benefits. It comes with sickness on
its wings, and rejoices only the doctor and
the sexton. When Charon hoists a sail, it
is the northeast that swells it ; it purveys
for famine and caters for pestilence. From
the savage realms of the Czar it comes
with desolating sweep, laden with moans *Laden with moans.*
from Siberian mines, and sounding like
echoes of the knout ; but not a fragrant
breath brings it from all the rosaries of

Persia, so destitute is it of grace and charity. While it reigns, no fire heats, no raiment comforts, no walls protect — cold without bracing, scorching without warmth. It deflowers the earth, and it wans the sky. The ghastliest of hues overspreads the face of things, and collapsing nature seems expiring of cholera. The cock in the barnyard is sullen and solitary; the horse in the stable has a whipped look; the donkey at the stack erects his ears, and shows metal in his heels; the pigeons moan, like the undercurrent of the brook; all men are shy and silent; the children are quarrelsome and perverse; the sparrows, even, are dumb and comfortless looking; engines groan with their loads, and spit spitefully their scalding steam; engineers see obstacles at every curve, and shiver; passengers snuggle poutingly into corners, and wonder if ever so many disagreeable people were in the same space before; the boy munches his apple with tenfold offensiveness; the baby misses the way to its mouth with its candied fist; the pug on the rug snaps and snarls like mad; marrow congeals; the spinal column gives sign of insecurity under the burden of a leaden brain. Alas, alas! A northeast wind must have been blowing

Nature seems expiring.

Engines groan.

Marrow congeals.

to account for an incident at a military exe- *Incident in Hyde Park*
cution in Hyde Park long ago — mentioned
by Gilly Williams.   A grave man, witnessing it, turned about, and said to a by-
stander, " By G—, I thought there was
more in it!"   And shot himself very soon
afterwards.   A northeast wind must have
been blowing to account for an event in *Event in Paris streets.*
Paris streets the day Robespierre was guil-
lotined — noted by Carlyle.   From the Pa-
lais de Justice to the Place de la Revolution, it is one dense stirring mass ; all
windows crammed ; the very roofs and
ridge-tiles budding forth curiosity, in strange
gladness.   All eyes are on Robespierre's *Robespierre's tumbril.*
tumbril, where he, his jaw bound in dirty
linen, with his half-dead brother, and half-
dead Henriot, lie shattered ; their seven-
teen hours of agony about to end.   The
gendarmes point their swords at him, to
show the people which he is.   A woman
springs on the tumbril ; clutching the side
of it with one hand ; waving the other sib-
yl-like ; and exclaims : " The death of thee
gladdens my very heart."   Robespierre
[thought by many to be dead] opened his *Opens his eyes.*
eyes : " Scoundrel ! Down to hell with the
curses of all wives and mothers !"   I can
imagine an east wind blowing when they

took Jesus out — bearing the cross for himself — to the place of a skull, and crucified him, between two thieves. I like to think of something to palliate the crime of Pilate and the mob. My Uncle Toby had a word to say for Satan, and Burns too, I think, in one of his poems.

Age and Want.

Age and Want, oh! ill-matched pair! A beggar was just now at the door — an old man. Seventy-five years of age, I should say, at least. The air was cold, and I did not encourage him to linger; though he did not seem inclined to relate a pitiful tale. He had evidently seen better days, and appeared to have a good deal of the pride of manhood left. There was nothing of obsequiousness in his manner, and the thankfulness he expressed was in the language of

Irish beggars.

self-respect and intelligence. The Irish beggars, as Thackeray describes them, come crawling round you with lying prayers and loathsome compliments, that make the stomach turn; they do not even disguise that they are lies; for, refuse them, and the wretches turn off with a laugh and a joke, a miserable grinning cynicism that creates distrust and indifference, and must be, one would think, the very best way to close the

purse, not to open it, for objects so un-
worthy. An old man, obliged to beg, is a
pitiable character. I do not like to think of
the extremity. Preserve, just Providence!
(exclaims Jean Paul) the old man from *Jean Paul's exclamation.*
want! for hoary years have already bent
him low, and he can no longer stand upright
with the youth, and bear heavy burdens on
his shoulders. I know of nothing more terrible to contemplate than the inconceiv-
able poverty and distress of the people of *The people of Thibet.*
Thibet, as described by a traveler in that
country. There are no plains save flats in
the bottoms of the valleys, and the paths
lead over lofty mountains. Sometimes,
when the inhabitants are obliged from famine to change their habitations in winter,
the old and feeble are frozen to death
standing and resting their chins on their
staves, remaining as pillars of ice, to fall *Men as pillars of ice.*
only when the thaw of the ensuing spring
commences! "Did you ever observe,"
asks Macdonald, in one of his novels, "that
there is not one word about the vices of
the poor in the Bible — from beginning to
end?" "We talk," said Douglas Jerrold,
"of the intemperance of the poor; why,
when we philosophically consider the crush-
ing miseries that beset them — the keen

The mockery of luxury.

suffering of penury, and the mockery of luxury and profusion with which it is surrounded — the wonder is, not that there are so many who purchase temporary oblivion of their misery, but that there are so few." The blessedness of life, remarks the Scotch author quoted, depends far more on its interest than upon its comfort. The need of exertion and the doubt of success render life much more interesting to the poor than it is to those who, unblessed with anxiety for the bread that perisheth, waste their poor hearts about rank and reputation. If men could discriminate between needs and wants, what fortunate changes would occur in their condition. Goldsmith wrote, "Man wants but little here below." Man needs but little here below, would have been nearer the truth. His necessities are few indeed ; his wants include everything. They are as hungry as his desires. Sense can support herself (says Carlyle) handsomely, in most countries, for some eighteen pence a day ; but for fantasy, planets and solar systems will not suffice. It is right that poverty in old age should be impressively held up to young people, and economy intelligently inculcated as the means to forefend it.

Life more interesting to the poor.

Carlyle.

"Ye immortal gods!" exclaimed Cicero; *Cicero.*
"men know not how great a revenue economy is." "Economy," said Voltaire, "is
the source of liberality." Thackeray, commending Macaulay's frugality, admonishes, *Macaulay's*
"To save be your endeavor, against the *frugality.*
night's coming, when no man may work;
when the arm is weary with long day's
labor; when the brain perhaps grows dark;
when the old, who can labor no more, want
warmth and rest, and the young ones call
for supper." An aged husbandman, as the
German allegory runs, was working in his *A German*
rich and wide-spread fields, at the decline *allegory.*
of day, when he was suddenly confronted
by a spectral illusion, in the form of a man.
"Who, and what are you?" said the astonished husbandman. "I am Solomon, the *Solomon, the*
wise," was the reply, "and I have come to *wise.*
inquire what you are laboring for?" "If
you are Solomon," said the husbandman,
"you ought to know that I am following
out the advice you have given. You referred me to the ant for instruction, and
hence my toil." "You have," said the ap-
parition, "learnt but half your lesson; I
directed you to labor in the proper season *The proper*
for labor, in order that you might repose *season for*
in the proper season for repose." *labor.*

I have been very wretched for the last
few days. Every ill, it seems to me, that
could afflict a man, has attacked me. Pains,
pains, the most searching and excruciating,
in every part of my miserable body. I
thought again and again that my poor
brain would split into pieces. The doctor
seemed attentive and anxious, and his powders and drops have brought me to a tolerable state again. And he himself continues
to be endurable, though he did last night
quote from one of the modern humorists —
there are dozens of them — who rely upon
extravagance, bad grammar, bad orthogra-
phy, and slang, to relieve the essential stu-
pidity of their pages. Seeing my blank
expression, he said, "You have n't read
him, perhaps." I did n't reply. The sagacious fellow, not to know my detestation
of such stuff! Still, he seems a good doctor, and reads to me sometimes, as a solace.
He is a natural reader. His reading is like
good talking. After his allusion to the
coarse humorist, he read to me, in a charm-
ing way, one of Zschokke's tales, and I for-
gave him. Again he declared his intention
to spend a long evening with me in my library, socially. I want to enlighten him a
little as to one thing. His limited means,

he thinks, will not permit him to purchase books, so, I suspect, he has fallen into the easily acquired habit of relying too much *An easily acquired habit.* upon newspapers and such books as fall in his way for intellectual food. He pleads a want of time too, and sets down to that his ignorance of good literature and defective literary taste. I hope, when I have the opportunity, to give him an object-lesson that will cure him effectually of his complaints. Ah! that searching pain in *A pain in his left elbow.* my left elbow! I can hardly hold the pen for the agony I suffer; but I must write a little now and then for occupation and variety. I cannot be always reading, and recording my pains. (Another book, for the doctor's special edification.) I feel myself about worn out. Everything distresses me. I am tired of the town, — man made it; I *Town and country.* pine for the country, — that God made. (Pope for authority.) Oh, the noises, the noises of the eternal Babel! The rattling milk-carts; the lumbering ice-wagons; the cries of the street-venders; the jingle of the bells of the horse-cars, day and night, that always seem to stop just before my door; the squeaking hand-organs; the infernal brass-bands; the roar and roar of *Roar of multitudinous wheels.* multitudinous wheels, wheels; the whirr of

the locomotive, like a hurricane, — thank
Heaven, several blocks away ; the dashing
state carriages till far into the early morning, when wise people should be asleep, —
at least be left undisturbed ; all together,
enough to hammer the brain into a jelly,
and destroy every vestige of humanity in
the soul.   How any one should be in love
with the town is past my comprehension.

Johnson and Macaulay infatuated with London. Johnson thought that when a man tired of
London he was tired of his life.   Macau-
lay was alike infatuated with London.
Jekyll used to say that, if compelled to live
in the country, he would have the road before his door paved like a street, and hire
a hackney-coach to drive up and down all

Lamb's aversion to the country. day.   Lamb had a like aversion to the
country, and pronounced a garden the prim-
itive prison, till man, with Promethean
felicity and boldness, luckily sinned himself out of it.   For my part, I hate the town
cordially, and — at times — everything in it.
The stock-subjects are detestable to me,
—the last fashion, the last actor, the last
dance, the last swindler, — in all of which
you are expected to be profoundly interested.   The cits will babble away to you
about evanescent nothings without limit.
I do not permit them.   And their devotion

and worship of Mammon! And how they *Worship of Mammon.*
submit to the few without a wish to escape
the despotism! The common individual
submits to be an atom, without responsibility or feeling. He is so small a part that he
feels no shame for the sins of the whole.
" Multitudes never blush." With Sterne,
in Tristram Shandy, I have the greatest
veneration in the world for that gentleman,
who, in distrust of his own discretion, sat
down and composed, at his leisure, fit
forms of swearing suitable for all cases, *Forms of swearing for all cases.*
from the lowest to the highest provoca-
tions, which could possibly happen to him;
which forms being well considered by him,
and such moreover as he could stand to,
he kept them ever by him on the chim-
ney-piece, within his reach, ready for use.
Think of it! an imprecation ever ready for
every annoyance of my detestable city life!
Capital idea! But as big a book it would *A capital idea.*
be as the Hermit of Bellyfulle's encyclo-
pedia of cookery, — who died, I believe,
after completing only a part of it, — a few
volumes only. Cities! How to account
for them! Charon, I think it was (in Lucian), who, surveying the earth one day
(from above) with Mercury — his one only
day of furlough under the bright sun —

Hiding-places. called them "hiding-places." **A** shrewd man sees a kettle **boil,** and others adapt the **thing called steam** to locomotive purposes; **and** forthwith, **one says, every** fool goes everywhere for what he calls his holidays, but which, indeed, are his most laborious days. Ultimately he sticks himself down in a place where he finds the greatest number **of people** like himself. Hence these huge

Contrast of fields and forests. cities! Ah, the contrast of fields and for- ests! Trees! **Think of them!** In the **United States thirty-six varieties of** oak, thirty-four **of pine, nine of fir, five** of spruce, four **of hemlock, two of** persimmon, twelve of ash, eighteen of willow, **nine of** poplar, **and I don't know how** many of the beauti-

Trees and leaves. ful beech. I once counted over thirty dif- ferent varieties of trees **in** the space of one acre. And the leaves! — their number, their individuality, their variety of shape and tint, the acres of space that those of one great tree would cover if spread out **and** laid together. **In the** autumn to watch them fall — **how slowly!** how rapidly! — **yet they say nobody ever saw** one of them let go! **Homer's** comparison to the lives of **men — how fine! Better** than Lucian's

An October day in Ohio. to the bubbles. I remember very well one October day in Ohio. It was long ago —

" In life's morning march, when my bosom
was young." (I like to quote from that
poem of Campbell's, — it is incomparable
of its kind.) A delightful tramp! Elder-
berries. (The great Boerhaave held the
elder in such pleasant reverence for the
multitude of its virtues, that he is said to
have taken off his hat whenever he passed
it.) Grapes. Haws. Papaws. (Nature's *Nature's*
custard.) Spicewood. Sassafras. Hickory *custard.*
nuts. Nearly a primeval forest. Vines
reminding one of Brazilian creepers. Trees
that were respectable saplings when Columbus landed. The dead roots of an iron-
wood — so like a monster as to startle.
Behemoth I thought of. ("He moveth his *Behemoth.*
tail like a cedar.") Thistle-down. Diffused
like small vices. Every seed hath wings.
Here and there a jay, or a woodpecker.
Grape vines, fantastically running over the
tops of tall bushes, — grouping deformi-
ties, any one of which, if an artist drew
it, would be called an exaggeration, worse
than anything of Doré's. Trees, swaying
and bowing to one another, like stilted *Stilted*
clowns in Nature's afterpiece of the Sea- *clowns.*
sons. Trees incorporated, — sycamore and
elm, maple and hickory, — modifying and
partaking each other's nature ; resembling

so much as to appear one tree. A jolly gray squirrel, — hopping from limb to limb, like a robin ; swinging like an oriole ; flying along the limb like a weaver's *A scudding cloud of pigeons.* shuttle ; scared away, at length, by a scudding cloud of pigeons, just brushing the tallest tree-tops, as if kissing an annual farewell. Clover. Sorrel. Pennyroyal. A drink of cider from a bit of broken crockery. ("Does he not drink more sweetly that takes his beverage in an earthen vessel than he that looks and searches into his golden chalices for fear of poison, and sleeps in armor, and trusts nobody, and does not trust God for his safety?") "All is fair — all glad, — from grass to *Not a melancholy day.* sun!" Not a "melancholy" day. Keats's poem on Autumn comes to mind ; and Crabbe's. "Welcome pure thoughts, welcome, ye silent groves ; these guests, these courts, my soul most dearly loves." Indian summer. Balzac's comparison to ripe womanhood. The significant worn walk round the mean man's field ; its crooked outline impressively striking. All in all, a white day. Memory of it supplies these notes. They might be expanded into an essay. The country, the country! Though the man who would truly relish and enjoy it (thought Dodsley in a letter to *To relish and enjoy the country.* Spence) must be previously furnished with a large and various stock of ideas, which he must be capable of turning over in his own mind, of comparing, varying, and contemplating upon with pleasure ; he must so thoroughly have seen the world as to cure him of being over fond of it ; and he must have so much good sense and virtue in his own heart as to prevent him from being disgusted with his own reflections, or uneasy in his own company. Alas ! —

The wits, most of them, have had their joke about the children. Sydney Smith, *Sydney Smith's joke about the children.* writing to Countess Grey of a new grandchild, says, " I am glad it is a girl; all little boys ought to be put to death." Lamb, *Lamb's.* after being plagued all the morning by noisy children, proposed a toast to "the memory of the m - m - much - abused and m-m-much calumniated good King Herod." A foolish woman once asked Barnes (editor *Barnes'.* of the London Times) whether he were fond of children, and received the answer, " Yes, ma'am ; boiled." Coleridge, in his fondness for them, called them " King- *Kingdom-of-Heavenites.* dom-of-Heavenites." Appropriate, I think, after spending a few minutes with a pretty little girl who brought me some fruit this morning. She was a lovely creature. In a plain dress of dark cloth ; roses in her cheeks ; sunshine in her hair ; innocence in her eyes ; in her face the light of heaven.

Father Ryan and the little child. Father Ryan, a Catholic priest, once told me how, while he was preaching, on a great occasion, a child he was fond of came suddenly inside the railing, and pulling at his robe, and looking up sweetly into his face, said, " Father Ryan, are you going to kith me ? " At which, of course, many in the great audience laughed. But when he took the darling up in his arms, and said, "Of such is the kingdom of heaven," and descanted upon the innocency and purity of childhood, there was not a dry eye in the church, and sobs not a few were distinctly heard in every part of the assembly. There is no doubt that children

Jean Paul. of a certain depth, as Jean Paul says, like buildings of a certain size, give echoes. Responses, we should call them, heard out of Paradise, repeated in the children.

Thackeray. " I love," says Thackeray, "to see the kind eyes of women fondly watching children as they gambol about ; a female face, be it ever so plain, when occupied in regarding children, becomes celestial almost, and a

man can hardly fail to be good and happy
while he is looking on such sights. 'Ah,
sir!' says an enormous *man, whom you
would not accuse of sentiment, 'I have a
couple of those things at home;' and he
stops and heaves a great big sigh and swallows down a half tumbler of cold something
and water.   We know what the honest fellow means well enough.   He is saying to
himself, 'God bless my girls and their
mother!'" "It is very easy," says Holmes,
in his remarkable Elsie Venner, "to criti-
cise other people's modes of dealing with
their children.   Outside observers see results; parents see processes.   They notice
the trivial movements and accents which
betray the blood of this or that ancestor;
they can detect the irrepressible movement of hereditary impulse in looks and
acts which mean nothing to the common
observer.   To be a parent is almost to be
a fatalist.   This boy sits with legs crossed,
just as his uncle used to whom he never
saw; his grandfathers both died before
he was born, but he has the movement of
the eyebrows which we remember in one
of them, and the gusty temper of the
other."   No wonder, said one who was
acquainted with Lady Byron as Miss Mil-

A couple of those things at home.

Other people's children.

To be a parent is to be a fatalist.

banke, that the marriage of Lord Byron was never one of reasonable promise. The bridegroom* and the bride were ill-assorted. They were two only children, and two spoilt children. The best way of training the young, that loftiest teacher of the ancients, Plato, said, is to train yourself at the same time ; not to admonish them, but to be always carrying out your own principles in practice. It was the conclusion of Professor Venable, one of the most accomplished of his profession, that many teachers of morality destroy the good effect of judicious counsel by too much talk, as a chemical precipitate is redissolved in an excess of the precipitating agent. "Train up a child in the way he should go : and when he is old he will not depart from it." "Generally speaking," thought Southey, " it will be found so ; but is there any other rule to which there are so many exceptions ? Ask the serious Christian, as he calls himself, or the professor (another and more fitting appellative which the Christian Pharisees have chosen for themselves), ask him whether he has found it hold good. Whether his sons, when they attained to years of discretion (which are the most indiscreet years in the course of human life),

Marginal notes:

Lord and Lady Byron.

Plato on training the young.

A mistake of teachers of morality.

Southey on training up children.

have profited as he expected by the long
extemporaneous prayers to which they listened night and morning, the sad Sabbaths *Sad Sab-*
baths.
which they were compelled to observe, and
the soporific sermons which closed the domestic religiosities of those melancholy
days. Ask them if this discipline has pre-
vented them from running headlong into
the follies and vices of the age, — from being bird-limed by dissipation, — or caught
in the spider's web of sophistry and unbe-
lief. 'It is no doubt a true observation,'
says Bishop Patrick, 'that the ready way *How to make*
minds grow
to make the minds of youth grow awry is *awry.*
to lace them too hard, by denying them
their just freedom.' Ask the old faithful
servant of Mammon, whom Mammon has
rewarded to his heart's desire, and in whom
the acquisition of riches has only increased
his eagerness for acquiring more, — ask
him whether he has succeeded in training
up his heir to the same service. He will
tell you that the young man is to be found *Experience*
of the ser-
upon race grounds, and in gaming-houses, *vant of*
Mammon.
that he is taking his swing of extravagance
and excess, and is on the high road to
ruin. Ask the wealthy Quaker [Southey
hated the Quakers], the pillar of the meeting — most orthodox in heterodoxy, — who

never wore a garment of forbidden cut or color, never bent his body in salutation, or his knees in prayer, — never uttered the heathen name of a day or month, nor ever addressed himself to any person without religiously speaking illegitimate English, *Converted by the tailor.* — ask him how it has happened that the tailor has converted his sons. He will fold his hands, and twirl his thumbs mournfully in silence. It has not been for want of training them in the way wherein it was his wish that they should go. You are about, sir, to send your son to a famous school. He may come from it an accomplished scholar to the utmost extent that school education can make him so ; he may be the better both for its discipline and its want of discipline ; it may serve him excel- *Doubtful results of school education.* lently well as a preparatory school for the world into which he is about to enter. But also he may come away an empty coxcomb or a hardened brute —a spendthrift — a profligate — a blackguard or a sot. To put a boy in the way he should go is like sending out a ship well found, well manned and stored, and with a careful captain ; but there are rocks and shallows in her course, winds and currents to be encountered, and all the contingencies and

perils of the sea." As to the training
and conduct of the children of my own
body, I choose to speak in the language of
John Buncle, who was seven times a hus- *John Buncle
band, and, one would infer, the father of a and his nu-
very numerous progeny. "As I mention," merous progeny.
he says, "nothing of any children by so
many wives, some readers may perhaps
wonder at this; and therefore, to give a
general answer, once for all, I think it suf-
ficient to observe, that I had a great many,
to carry on the succession; but as they
never were concerned in any extraordinary affairs, nor ever did any remarkable
things, that I heard of, only rise and breakfast, read and saunter, drink and eat, it
would not be fair, in my opinion, to
trouble any one with their history."

Is life worth living? Pecuniarily, hard- *Is life worth
ly, one would think, to very many, after living?
reading Dr. Farr's interesting chapter on
the pecuniary value of life. A certain
amount of expense, he says, has to be in-
curred in any class before a child can attain
such an age and such strength that it can
earn its own livelihood. It is very difficult
to estimate what the expenses of even a
careful man who passes through the ordi-

nary university career must have been before he is able to earn anything for himself.
Among the lower ranks the problem is
simpler, though the facts and the general
course of events have, making due allow-
ance for difference in station, a considerable similarity. The value, says the doctor,
of any class of lives is determined by valu-
ing first at birth, or at any age, the cost
of future maintenance ; and then the value
of the future earnings.   Thus proceeding,
I found the value of a Norfolk agricultural
laborer to be £246 at the age of twenty-
five ; the child is by this method worth
only £5 at birth ; £56 at the age of five ;
£117 at the age of ten ; the youth £192
at the age of fifteen ; the young man £234
at the age of twenty ; the man £246 at
the age of twenty-five ; £241 at the age of
thirty, when the value goes on declining to
£136 at the age of fifty-five ; and only one
pound at the age of seventy ; the cost of
maintenance afterwards exceeding the earnings, the value becomes negative ; at eighty
the value of the cost of maintenance ex-
ceeds the value of the earnings by £41.

The stupid doctors.

The stupid doctors, little as they know,
it must be admitted, have made some ad-

*The pecuni-
ary value of
life.*

*At seventy
the value
becomes
negative.*

vance since Hippocrates. One of the court physicians, in the reign of Charles II., invented an instrument to cleanse the stomach and wrote a pamphlet on it ; and ridiculous as a stomach scrubbing-brush may appear, it afterward got a place among surgical instruments, and received a Latin name, meaning cleanser of the stomach ; but the moderns not having stomach for it have transferred it to the wine-merchant, who more appropriately applies it to the scouring of the interior of bottles. Heister gives a minute description of it. Many of the remedies recommended and recorded by the great and good Sir Thomas Browne are not a bit less ridiculous or absurd than those mentioned in the compilation following. There was a special water procured by distillation from a peck of garden shell snails and a quart of earth worms, besides other things ; this was prescribed, not for consumption alone, but for dropsy and all obstructions. For broken bones, bones out of joint, or any grief in the bones or sinews, oil of swallows was pronounced exceedingly sovereign, and this was to be procured by pounding twenty live swallows in a mortar with about as many different herbs ! A mole, male or female according

A stomach scrubbing-brush.

For consumption.

to the sex of the patient, was to be dried in an oven whole as taken out of the earth, and administered in powder for the epilepsy. A gray eel, with a white belly, was to be inclosed in an earthen pot, and buried alive in a dung-hill, and at the end of a

To help hearing. fortnight its oil might be collected to "help hearing." A mixture of rose leaves and pigeon's dung quilted in a bag, and laid hot upon the parts affected, was thought to

For the quinsy. help a stitch in the side ; and for the quinsy, "give the party to drink," says one of the old books, " the herb mouse-ear, steeped in ale or beer ; and look when you see a swine rub himself, and there upon the same place rub a slick stone, and then with it slick all

To make the hair grow. the swelling, and it will cure it." To make hair grow on a bald part of the head, garden snails were to be plucked out of their houses, and pounded with horse leeches, bees, wasps, and salt, an equal quantity of each ; and the baldness was to be anointed with a moisture from this mixture after it had been buried eight days in a hotbed.

To remove hair. For the removal and extirpation of superfluous hairs, a depilatory was to be made by drowning in a pint of wine as many green frogs as it would cover (about twenty was the number), setting the pot forty days in

the sun, and then straining it for use. A
water specially good against gravel or *For dropsy.*
dropsy might be distilled from the dried
and pulverized blood of a black buck or he-
goat, three or four years old. The animal
was to be kept by himself, in the summer-
time when the sun was in Leo, and dieted
for three weeks upon certain herbs given
in prescribed order, and to drink nothing
but red wine, if you would have the best
preparation, though some persons allowed
him his fill of water every third day. But
there was a water of man's blood, which *Water of*
in Queen Elizabeth's days was a new in- *man's blood.*
vention, "whereof some princes had very
great estimation, and used it for to remain
thereby in their force, and, as they thought,
to live long." A strong man was to be
chosen, in his flourishing youth, and of
twenty-five years, and somewhat choleric
by nature. He was to be well dieted for
one month with light and healthy meats,
all kinds of spices, good strong wine, and,
moreover, "kept with mirth;" at the *To be kept*
month's end, veins in both arms were *with mirth.*
opened, and as much blood let out as he
could "tolerate and abide." One handful
of salt was added to six pounds of this
blood, and this was seven times distilled,

pouring the water upon the residuum after every distillation, till the last. This was to be taken three or four times a year, an ounce at a time.

An ounce at a time.

Diseased sensibility is one of my worst maladies. I suffer from it, at times, as no mortal could know. It takes every form of mental misery. Now I am down to a point so low that the machinery of thinking all stops; again I just touch insanity itself, where the mental machinery is all ready to fly to pieces. Noises, scarcely heard by another, pain me to the limit of distress. In every nerve and fibre I tremble in terror, and my scared faculties lose all power of resistance. I envy, from my soul, the Lapp who drinks tobacco oil as a stomachic, and has a skin as insensible as his stomach. In Lapland, as Montesquieu puts it, " you must flay a man to make him feel." I can well understand the sensitiveness of Lord Byron, who, even in dying, shrunk away when those about him put their hands near his foot, as if fearing that they should uncover it. In his last sickness it was thought right to apply blisters to the soles of his feet. When on the point of putting them on, the poet asked the attendant whether it

His scared faculties lose all power of resistance.

Byron when dying.

would answer the purpose to apply both on *The poet's suggestion.*
the same leg. Guessing immediately the
motive that led him to ask this question, the
nurse told him that he would place them
above the knees. " Do so," was the reply.
I once knew a man — eminent in his profession — who carried an unsightly birth-
mark in his face. I never met him without
perceiving a slight shock of apprehension,
lest I might observe too closely his misfortune. Dr. Franklin mentions a gentleman
who, having one very handsome and one
shriveled leg, was wont to test the dispo- *A novel test of disposi-*
sition of a new acquaintance by observing *tion.*
whether he or she looked first or most at the
best or worst leg. Erskine was intensely
sensitive, and his acute sensibility being in-
dependent of any and every other malady,
as my sensitiveness is not (to my everlasting distress), it helped him as an advo-
cate and orator. Once, we are told, he was
confused and put out in an impassioned
address to a jury by a yawning attorney,
placed by malice prepense exactly in his line *Malice pre-*
of view under the jury-box. Arrested in *pense.*
his own despite by the absent or desponding
look of Garrow, who was with him in the
cause, he whispered," Who do you think can
get on with that wet blanket of a face of

Erskine's maiden effort. yours before him ? " His maiden effort in the House of Commons was marred by the real or affected indifference of Pitt, who, after listening a few minutes, and taking a note or two as if intending to reply, dashed pen and paper upon the floor with a contemptuous smile. Erskine could not recover from this expression of disdain ; " his voice faltered, he struggled through the remainder of his speech, and sank into his seat dispirited and shorn of his fame." On

Pitt's bitterness. another occasion, Pitt rose after Erskine and began : " I rise to reply to the right honorable gentleman (Fox) who spoke last but one. As for the honorable and learned gentleman who spoke last, he did no more than regularly repeat what fell from the gentleman who preceded him, and as regularly weakened what he repeated." No man ever existed, I believe, with more acute and unavoidable antipathies than my-

A story told by Lamb. self. I can well believe the story told by Charles Lamb, of two persons meeting (who never saw each other before in their lives) and instantly fighting. Blank, said Coleridge, " is one of those men who go far to shake my faith in a future state of existence ; I mean on account of the difficulty of knowing where to place him. I could not bear to roast him ; he is not so bad as all *Not bad enough to be roasted.* that comes to : but then, on the other hand, to have to sit down with such a fellow in the very lowest pot-house of heaven is utterly inconsistent with the belief of that place being a place of happiness for me." There are men who bully me with their immense, swaggering, animal spirits ; and I can imagine the distress of the sensitive Goldsmith in the presence of the high-fed, *Goldsmith and Foote.* gigantic, aggressive Foote. That element of Macaulay's character, which Palmerston called "cock-sureness," must have had much the same effect upon shrinking and self-distrusting natures brought in contact with it. Thoms, the founder and long the editor of Notes and Queries, met Lord Macaulay in the House of Lords one day, *Anecdote of Macaulay.* and remarked that he could not quite understand why Pope satirized Dryden in the Dunciad. Macaulay replied that Thoms must be mistaken, and before an audience of a score of peers spoke with his usual energy and eloquence in support of his view that Pope could not and would not have lampooned Dryden. All this time Thoms had a copy of the Dunciad in his pocket with a leaf turned down at the passage to which he had referred, but he was too well bred to produce the volume. Sydney Smith said of Richard Lovell Edgeworth, *Fuddled with animal spirits.* "He is fuddled with animal spirits, giddy with constitutional joy." Such a man to come into the presence of another all quivering from the effects of every malady known under the sun is a calamity. One objection that I have to my new doctor is that he has too high health. The mercury at zero, he comes steaming in like a locomotive. His features blaze like a constellation. And he is a little bit unceremonious, too, at times. Courtesy we expect, and have a right to, in a fair degree; in the *Courtesy a commodity.* doctor it is a commodity — we pay for it. To the point of obeisance or obsequiousness, however, it is as offensive as brusqueness or boorishness. Mrs. Basil Montagu met Burns, and pronounced him "the most royally courteous of mankind." In his sense of manhood he never forgot the man. In that portrait of Nasmyth's he carries *Burns a natural gentleman.* the brow and mien of a natural gentleman. Ah, a gentleman! A rarer thing, thought Thackeray, than some of us think for. Which of us can point out many such in his circle, — men whose aims are generous, whose truth is constant and elevated; who can look the world honestly in the face, with an equal manly sympathy for the great and *Great and small alike to him.* the small ? We all know a hundred whose coats are well made, and a score who have excellent manners ; but of gentlemen how many ? Let us take a little scrap of paper and each make out his list. An amusing illustration of obeisance is in that most grotesque figure in Serjeant Ballantine's book of Experiences, of a decently dressed, quiet-looking man who used to present himself *A grotesque scene.* after dinner to the judges and counsel on the last day of the Old Bailey sessions. Upon his appearance he was always presented with a glass of wine, and this he drank to the health of his patrons, expressing " with becoming modesty his gratitude for past favors and his hopes for favors to come." It was Calcraft, the hangman ! In contrast with that is the royal language of Byron, in one of his Dedications. After the words " Scott alone," Byron inserted, in a parenthesis, — " He will excuse the Mr. — we do not say Mr. Cæsar." Good- *Good-breeding a gift of God.* breeding is not wholly acquired ; to some extent, like genius, it is the gift of God. When two persons of exceptional good-breeding (says Holmes) meet in the midst of the common multitude, they seek each other's company at once by the natural law

Elective affinities. of elective affinities. It is wonderful how men and women know their peers. If two strange queens, sole survivors of two ship-wrecked vessels, were cast, half-naked, on a rock together, each would at once address the other as " Our Royal Sister." Louis *Louis XIV. and Lord Stair.* XIV. was told that Lord Stair was one of the best-bred men in Europe. " I shall soon put him to the test," said the king ; and asking Lord Stair to take an airing with him, as soon as the door of the coach was opened, he bade him pass and get in. The other bowed and obeyed. The king said, " The world is in the right, in the character it gives — another person would have troubled me with ceremony."

Politeness of Louis XIV. It has been said that never was man so polite as Louis XIV. He never passed a woman, however lowly her position, even though she were one of the menials of his palace, without raising his hat, and the whole time he conversed with a lady he remained uncovered. And yet never was man more selfish and indifferent to the convenience of both man and woman ; no matter what might be the state of the weather, no matter how delicate might be their health, he insisted upon all the la-

dies of the court attending him in his long Selfishness incarnate.
drives or promenades, sometimes continued
through several hours, beneath a burning
sun or in frost and snow. Sometimes they
fell fainting from their horses with illness,
or fatigue, but such incidents never moved
him. "Tell Murray," said Sydney Smith
to Jeffrey, "that I was much struck with
the politeness of Miss Markham the day
after he went. In carving a partridge, I
splashed her with gravy from head to foot;
and though I saw three distinct brown rills
of animal juice trickling down her cheek,
she had the complaisance to swear that not
a drop had reached her!" I have heard Mr.
Fraser say (says Wraxall, in his Historical
Memoirs), who was, during many years,
under-secretary of state, that in 1760, a few
months before the king died, having occasion to present a paper to him for his sig-
nature, at Kensington, George the Second *George II.*
took the pen in his hand; and having, as
he conceived, affixed his name to it, returned it to Fraser. But so defective was
his vision, that he had neither dipped his
pen in the ink, nor did he perceive that of
course he had only drawn it over the paper,
without making any impression. Fraser, *Fraser's delicacy.*
aware of the king's blindness, yet unwill-

ing to let his majesty observe that he discovered it, said, "Sir, I have given you so
bad a pen, that it will not write. Allow me
to present you a better for the purpose."
Then dipping it himself in the ink, he returned it to the king, who, without making
any remark, instantly signed the paper. It
is said that towards a chancellor whom Sir
Sugden and Edward Sugden liked he could be as sweet
Cottenham. as summer. Lord Cottenham one day fell
asleep on the bench. Sir Edward immediately paused. The cessation of sound
had the customary effect of awakening the
chancellor. "Why don't you go on, Sir Edward?" "I thought your lordship might
be looking over your notes," was the bland
response. This, of course, pleased the chancellor, who was liable to doze, and hated
Greeley. anybody noticing it. Horace Greeley said
he had never been beaten in politeness but
once. That happened, he said, many years
before. Early one morning he left Bragg's
Hotel, at Utica, in the stage-coach, west-
ward bound. There was but one passenger
besides himself, — a gentleman of very pre-
possessing appearance, with whom he soon
fell into conversation. After a while the
stranger slowly and, as it were, mechani-
cally drew a cigar-case from his pocket, and,

opening it, tendered it to Mr. Greeley, who declined the kind offer. The conversation *Declines a cigar.* was resumed; and presently the stranger, extracting a cigar from the case, placed it in his mouth, and returned the case to his pocket. Another interval of talk ensued, when the stranger abruptly but deferentially remarked to Mr. Greeley, "I hope, sir, you have no objection to a cigar?" "None in the world, sir," replied Mr. Greeley, "when it is not alight." "Oh," said his companion, "I had not the most remote thought of lighting it." There- *Conquered in politeness.* upon Mr. Greeley felt that he had been conquered in politeness.

As to compliments, I employ myself recollecting a few that are remarkable in literature. It was told of Lord Ashbrook, who never touched a feather during an entire day's shooting at Holkham, that the keeper, by way of consolation, remarked that he had seen people shoot worse than his lordship. "How can that be when I have missed bird after bird?" "Ay, but *An amusing compliment.* your lordship misses them so clean!" After his overthrow, Hannibal took refuge at the court of Prusias, King of Bithynia. There Scipio came on an embassy. The two great rivals met, and in conversation Scipio asked Hannibal whom he considered the greatest commander. "Alexander," was the reply. "And who next?" "Pyrrhus." "And who after him?" "Myself." "And what would you have said if you had beaten me at Zena?" "In that case I should have put myself before Alexander and Pyrrhus and all other generals." Mademoiselle Ra-

chel was very anxious to have her portrait taken by Ingres, and made an appointment with him at his studio to talk the matter over. In the course of conversation he remarked that in order to do justice to his model he should require at least fifty sittings of from two to three hours each. "How long will it be before the portrait is completed?" she inquired. "Four or five years," was the painter's reply. "Misery!" exclaimed Rachel; "then I must abandon the idea, for I may be dead and buried before you have immortalized me." "Mademoiselle," answered Ingres, with a smile, "I have no such pretension; your own genius has already saved me the trouble."

Allen, one of Leigh Hunt's school-fellows, was so handsome, that running one day against a barrow-woman in the street, and turning round to appease her in the midst

of her abuse, she said, "Where are you
driving to, you great hulking, good-for-
nothing, beautiful fellow, God bless you!"
Voltaire, being on a visit to a very lovely *Voltaire.*
woman, said to her, "Your rivals are the
curious works of art; you are the most complete work of nature." Dr. Johnson paid a
fine compliment to the wife of Dr. Beattie,
when he wrote to Boswell, "Of Dr. Beattie *Johnson to Boswell.*
I should have thought much, but that his
lady puts him out of my head; she is a very
lovely woman." Colley Cibber alluded to *Colley Cibber.*
the Duchess of Marlborough as possessing
something that distinguished her above all
the women of her time, — a distinction
which she received not from earthly sover-
eigns, but "from the Author of Nature;"
that of being "a great-grandmother with- *Duchess of Marl-borough.*
out gray hairs." But the most extravagant
compliment — the most magnificent display of gallantry — is recorded by Madame
de Genlis, in her Memoirs. Madame de
Blot, then very young, one day said in the
presence of the Prince of Conti, that she
wished to have the portrait of her canary
in a ring. The prince offered to give her
the portrait and the ring, which Madame *Madame de Blot.*
de Blot accepted, on condition that the ring
should be mounted in the simplest manner,

The ring. and not set with stones. The ring was, in fact, only a hoop of gold, but instead of a glass to cover the portrait, a large diamond had been used, which was ground as thin as glass. Madame de Blot discovered this piece of prodigality, and returned the diamond ; upon which the Prince of Conti caused the diamond to be ground into powder, and used it to dry the ink of the letter *The prince's gallantry.* he wrote on the subject to Madame de Blot. And so I run on in a rambling way, dwelling on pleasant things in my library, as a resource and remedy for my desperate malady. But I cannot close my record of the day without referring to an incident pleasanter than any I have cited to a man in my lone, lorn, miserable condition — mentioned by Dr. Johnson. " I knew, " *A very pretty instance.* said the doctor, " a very pretty instance of a little girl, of whom her father was very fond, who once when he was in a melancholy fit, and had gone to bed, persuaded him to rise in good humor by saying, ' My dear papa, please to get up, and let me help you on with your clothes, that I may learn to do it when you are an old man.' " Ah ! solar systems for such a child !

Lord Chancellor Brougham was once

asked to define a lawyer. "A lawyer," he *Brougham's definition of a lawyer.* said, "is a learned gentleman who rescues your estate from your enemies and keeps it himself." My observation and experience, too, prove to me the truthfulness of the definition. My agent came to me yesterday to say that the claim left in the hands of a lawyer in Illinois for collection is lost! — the rascal having pocketed the amount, in addition to moneys from time to time advanced to him as fees. The villainy is a surprise and a great vexation, *An unpleasant surprise.* for the reason that the rascal was highly recommended to me for probity and honor. How many comforts that thousand dollars or so would have bought me! How many physician's visits and apothecary's bills it would have paid! The debtor, it appears, was an honest man ; the incorruptible attorney employed to hunt him down turns *The lawyer the thief.* out to be the thief. Time was when such villainy might have been punished. Not now. The profession stand together for mutual protection. Now and then an effort is made to disbar an attorney for criminal practices, and as often it fails. Dealing so habitually in tricks and perjuries, the feeble promptings and declarations of truth are unfelt and unheeded. It was

Caleb Balderstone, I believe, the faithful
seneschal at Wolf's Crag, that was always
telling "lees" for the "credit of the family." So the legal profession, quarrel as
they may and do, amongst themselves, —
saying things to one another that go to
the sources of character, — are nevertheless always ready in words of excuse, defense, and approbation of one another.
No matter how many estates they swallow
up, they are innocency incarnate. The fly
once into the parlor of the spider, it is the
holy of holies. And the spiders are in
league with one another. They inveigle
to ruin. Peterborough is made to say by
Landor, and very justly, "If an English
lawyer is in danger of starving in a mar-
ket-town or village, he invites another, and
both thrive." The more the better. They
inspire quarrels, and grow rich settling
them. They suggest the indispensable
testimony, and it is supplied. "I want to
go into a coal-mine," said Tom Sheridan,
"in order to say I have been there."
"Well, then, say so," replied the admirable
father. Lying is so easy, and is so freely
excused. "To lie for a friend," said Voltaire, "is friendship's first duty. Lying is
a vice only when it does harm ; it is a very

*Caleb Bal-
derstone.*

*Peter-
borough.*

Lying.

great virtue when it does good." There is
a story of an Irishman on his trial for a
felony who brought witnesses to speak for
his character. They bore their testimony
but too effectually, — the catalogue of the
novel virtues which were attributed to him
so perplexed his imagination that he cried
out in court, "My lord, if I had but known
what I was, I would not have done it!"
The effect was just as surprising but very
different in a case of Serjeant Ballantine's,
reported in his interesting Experiences.
One of his first briefs was given to him by
a rather shady attorney of the Jewish per-
suasion : and being at that time without
experience, young Ballantine yielded im-
plicitly to his instructions. A young gentleman of the same faith, he says, was
called as a witness. My client suggested
a question. Blindly I put it, and was
met by a direct negative. "What a lie!"
ejaculated my client, and dictated another
question : the same result followed, and
a similar ejaculation. By his further instruction I put a third, the answer to
which completely knocked us over. My
client threw himself back. "Well," said
he, "he is a liar, he always was a liar, and
always will be a liar." "Why," remarked

I, "you seem to know all about him."
"Of course I do," was the reply; "he is
my own son!"   Lying, says Leigh Hunt,
is the commonest and most conventional
of all the vices. It pervades, more or less,
every class of the community, and is fancied to be so necessary to the carrying
on of human affairs, that the practice is
tacitly agreed upon ; nay, in other terms,
openly avowed. In the monarch, it is
kingcraft. In the statesman, expediency.
In the churchman, mental reservation. In
the lawyer, the interest of his client. In
the merchant, manufacturer, and shop-
keeper, secrets of trade. Says Taine, the
best of men in Paris lie ten times a day ;
the best of women twenty times a day ;
the fashionable man a hundred times a
day. No estimate has ever been made as
to how many times a day a fashionable
woman lies. Father Holt, the Jesuit, in
Esmond, said to the boy, Henry, "that
if to keep silence is not to lie, as it certainly is not, yet silence is, after all, equiv-
alent to a negation, and therefore a down-
right No, in the interest of justice or your
friend, and in reply to a question that may
be prejudicial to either, is not criminal, but
on the contrary, praiseworthy ; and as law-

Lying.

Secrets of trade.

Father Holt.

ful a way as the other of eluding a wrong-
ful demand." The bad in human nature *The bad in human nature.*
is generously accommodated. There are
good and bad notes in most voices, it is
said — I know little about it myself. On
one occasion, in Italy, a composer wrote
his solos for one of his opera singers in a
way to bring in all his worst notes very
frequently; but it was to get rid of him.
Happy if the exposure of evil in the legal *Professional evil.*
profession resulted in the same manner.
But hired sin becomes brazen, and virtue,
as a consequence, shamefaced. It has
been remarked as a noticeable fact that all
contributions to the "conscience fund"
are made anonymously. Can it be, it has
been asked, that the man with a conscience is ashamed of it? Too tender a
conscience has been remarked upon by
Goethe as objectionable. He spoke of a
boy who could not console himself after
he had committed a trifling fault. "I was
sorry to observe this," said Goethe, "for *Goethe on a too tender conscience.*
it shows a too tender conscience, which
values so highly its own moral self that it
will excuse nothing in it." Such a conscience, he thought, makes unhealthy characters, if it is not balanced by great activity. Two consciences are suggested as

*Two con-
sciences ob-
served by
Talleyrand.* useful by Talleyrand. A distinguished personage remarked to him, " In the upper chamber at least are to be found men possessed of consciences." "Consciences," replied Talleyrand, "to be sure : I know many a peer who has got two." Society grows more and more lenient towards vil-*Statutes and
penalties.* lainy. Statutes, more and more, are being framed by the criminal lawyers for the benefit of criminals. Penalties, too, are being lessened and lessened. A breach of verbal contract is not any very great matter in these days of universal enlightenment and much preaching ; but think of the penalty for it in the Zendavesta — liability of the next of kin to the ninth degree, and three hundred years in hell !

*The first
lawyer.* The first lawyer, I believe, that we have any account of in Holy Writ is Jonadab, who is described by the inspired writer as a "very subtile man." He was consulted by Amnon in the sin against Tamar his sister. He was an arch pettifogger, I have no doubt. He gave the devilish advice and disappeared from the scene. Jonadab, the "subtile man : " a fair type, I should think, of too great a proportion of the lawyers *Hypocritical
priests and
corrupt
judges.* — next in the order of approximate total depravity to the hypocritical priests and

corrupt judges. A convenient, elastic conscience, subtilty, and what is vulgarly
called "cheek," are indispensable. "I
would rather have your cheek," said a gentleman to a petty attorney, "than a license
to steal." Any way to accomplish an object ; but the audacious or cunning way,
being most professional, is preferred. In
their covert practices they sometimes re-
mind me of the blood-sucking bats of South *Blood-suck-*
America, described by Wallace. The ex- *ing bats.*
act manner in which the animal attacks is
not positively known, as the sufferer never
feels the wound. The motion of the wings
fans the sleeper into a deeper slumber, and
renders him insensible to the gentle abra-
sion of the skin either by teeth or tongue.
Thus ultimately forms a minute opening,
the blood flowing from which is sucked or
lapped up by the hovering vampire. "Keep *Advice of*
out of chancery," said old Krook, in *old Krook.*
Bleak House. "For," said he, "it 's being
ground to bits in a slow mill ; it 's being
roasted at a slow fire ; it 's being stung to
death by single bees ; it 's being drowned
by drops ; it 's going mad by grains." As
to advocacy, I have long thought with
Carlyle, that it is a strange trade. "Your
intellect, your highest heavenly gift, hung

up in the shop-window like a loaded pistol
for sale ; will either blow out a pestilent
scoundrel's brains, or the scoundrel's salu-
tary sheriff's officer's (in a sense), as you
please to choose for your guinea." Sometimes, in a generous mood, I am reminded of Paddy's suggestion of economy
in justice, and feel like commending it as a
stroke of policy. It occurred in the case
of an outlaw, who was a blacksmith, con-
demned to transportation for life, but who
excited powerful sympathy on the score
of his professional merits. He lived in a
hunting county where his aid was thought
so valuable that an application was made
to the judge in order that his sentence
might be mitigated. "He is the only
man, your honor," said the influential dep-
utation, "who can shoe a horse for miles
about us." "Impossible, gentlemen," replied the Rhadamanthus; "an example
must be made." "Very true," observed
the applicants ; "but, you see, we have got
only one blacksmith, whilst we have a
number of attorneys. Could n't you take
one of the attorneys ?" Though commending the suggestion, I am happy to record that I know at least one lawyer who
is an honest man. His big brain is the

*Economy in
justice.*

*Implacable
Rhadaman-
thus.*

home of wisdom, and "the Ten Commandments are written on his countenance."

Integrity, entireness, soundness to the *Integrity.*
core. I do like an honest man. He re-
alizes the precept, in passing every day as
the last, and in being neither violently excited nor torpid, nor playing the hypocrite. He stands a man, responsible to
all men for all the manhood there is in
him. He is known and read, and his life
is in no sense a lie. He so lives with man
"as considering that God sees him, and so
speaks to God as if men heard him." "I
look upon the simple and childish virtues
of veracity and honesty," says Emerson, *Veracity*
and honesty
"as the root of all that is sublime in character. Speak as you think, be what you
are, pay your debts of all kinds. I prefer
to be owned as sound and solvent, and my
word as good as my bond, and to be what
cannot be skipped, or dissipated, or under-
mined, to all the éclat in the universe."
Society could not exist for a day without
moral honesty ; it is as the hair in the *Moral hon-*
esty.
mortar which holds the elements together.
There must be integrity, if everything is
not to be artificial and conventional. General Thomas said that the prime essential

You must tell the truth to the Indians. in dealing with the Indians was to tell the truth, to tell the truth always, and to keep a promise, because to the white man when you failed to keep a promise you could give an apology that might be compre-hended, but the Indian never understood if you did not keep your agreement. Va-lerius records that Fabius redeemed cer-tain captives by the promise of a sum of money ; which when the senate refused to confirm, he sold all the property he pos-sessed, and with the produce paid down the stipulated sum, caring less to be poor in lands than poor in honesty. Confucius *A saying of Confucius.* said, " At first, my way with men was to hear their words, and give them credit for their conduct. Now, my way is to hear their words, and look at their conduct." " They that cry down moral honesty," said old John Selden, " cry down that which is a great part of religion, my duty towards God, and my duty towards man. What care I to see a man run after a sermon, if he cozens and cheats as soon as he comes *Religion without moral hon-esly* home ? " Religion were emptiness and pretence without moral honesty ; and only sentimentalists and illuminists in religion denounce it. When a preacher, of good sense, fairly upon his feet, inveighs against morality, I set it down mathematically that he is either uncandid or mercenary. I have noticed that such (when not irresponsible from enthusiasm) almost invariably illustrated their discourses in a way unconsciously to denote their irrepressible, constitutional thrift; and threatened to resign their pastorates if their salaries were not promptly paid. It was apparent enough that they knew perfectly well that houses are not built by beginning at the roof; yet they reasoned preposterously that characters could be built in that absurd manner. Balloons, that move with the air, are not structures to resist the tempests; temples, that outlast the storm, have rock foundations. At the bottom of the edifice which is destined to stand, and to show no crack or flaw for ages, are great, invisible, well-dressed stones, perfectly leveled, and perfectly laid in cement. So at the foundation of the character of every honest man there are virtues and elements, cemented and established, that are destined to make it worthily everlasting. They are invisible, and were not for a moment thought of as to be seen by the architect. The honest man feels himself continually searched by the eye of

What he had noticed.

At the foundation of every honest man.

God, and the observation and estimate of the world are of secondary importance to him. He distinguishes between the real *Substance* substance, character, and its shadow, repu- *and shadow.* tation. He is careful about repeating the Lord's Prayer, as he cannot help regarding it as a test of himself, as well as an act of adoration to the Deity. Before pronouncing the words, Forgive us our debts, as we also have forgiven our debtors, he hesitates, and inquisition begins. *Conscience* Conscience dons the ermine, and con- *and con-* sciousness testifies. Conceit of superex- *sciousness.* cellence is not a natural result of such self-examination. The ideal seems further from attainment with every effort ; but effort is encouraged to become habitual by increased sense of responsibility. An individual, not responsible to party or sect, he has a conscience directly toward God. Doing his best to live virtuously and walk humbly, he confidently trusts the Creator to take care of the creature. With the highest standards of conduct practicable or attainable, he judges himself not less *The Golden* severely than others. The Golden Rule *Rule.* he believes to be particularly for self-application. His moral anchorages are fixed and habitual. There are things that un-

der no possible circumstances would he
do. His principles are in such constant *Principles and instincts.*
use that they have the look of instincts.
His morals are so constantly applied that
they have the appearance of habits. He
has realized the precept of Plutarch, that
habit soon makes right conduct easy.
Habit, indeed, he has discovered to be
omnipotent. "All is habit," says Metastasio, — "even virtue itself." In brutes,
even, he has seen the controlling effect of
discipline. It is related that during the
Franco-German war, after the slaughter at
Vionville, a strange and touching spectacle *A touching spectacle.*
was presented. On the evening call being
sounded by the first regiment of Dragoons
of the Guard, six hundred and two rider-
less horses answered to the summons, —
jaded, and in many cases maimed. The
noble animals still retained their disciplined habits. But deeper than discipline
or habit — far down below either — the
character of a thoroughly honest man takes
root. Hawthorne said of his trusted as-
sistant in the custom-house at Salem, that
his integrity was a law of nature with him *Integrity a law of nature.*
rather than a choice or a principle. The
life of the thoroughly honest man, as I
have said, is in no sense a lie. His acts

Acts and professions.

are better than his professions. He performs, if possible, his promises. In a public or fiduciary capacity he acts as if his responsibilities were personal. He does not turn thief when elected to office. He does not sink his soul in a corporation. He knows no friend in court. He does not deliberately swallow up estates by manipulating weak judges and procuring straw-bail, and afterward mercifully call the attention of the Almighty to the sins and short-comings of the women and children and imbeciles he has swindled and ruined. He does not live and flourish at a great rate at others' expense. The dollar in his pocket is not his if he owes any man a dollar. Scrupulous in meeting his obligations, he is careful about incurring them. Patches on his clothing are of little moment compared with blotches of discredit on his character. If by fraud or an act of God his affairs have suffered, his creditors are the first to be notified. He does not go on from bad to worse till his neighbors who have trusted him are cheated and confounded. He does not with the wheels of his equipage splash the mud of the streets upon poor pedestrians, when his whole effects would pay only a small part of his

Awful hypocrisy.

Conduct in extremity.

indebtedness. He makes a clean breast *Fair to all alike.* to his butcher and baker, as well as to his banker, that neither may have any advantage over the other. He takes no advantage of oversight or neglect, and meets misfortune more than half way. His precepts and practices agree. If he or one of his children finds a sum of money, the act is not so hidden as to make it a theft. He will not have one penny that is not his — that cannot be accounted for. Clean hands, a clean conscience. There is a story of an old merchant who, on his death- *Death-bed of an honest man.* bed, divided the result of long years of labor, some few hundreds in all, amongst his sons. "It is little enough, my boys," were almost his last words, "but there is n't a dirty shilling in the whole of it."

Every man with a generous share of good blood in him begins life a democrat and a reformer. "I am no more ashamed of having been a republican," says Southey, *Sayings of Southey and Lord Eldon.* "than I am of having been a child." Lord Eldon said in his old age, that "if he were to begin life again, he would be damned but he would begin as agitator." There was a time in my own life when making the whole world over seemed to me not a very difficult or gigantic thing.

For six weeks a reformer.
For as much as six whole weeks the process seemed very simple and easy. All that was requisite, it appeared to me, was for the sinless to get together and determine upon a plan to convert the sinful, — to make them sinless as themselves. Simplicity itself! and as practicable as easy. The good had only to agree upon the manner of making over the bad, and the work was accomplished, — neatly, and with dispatch. An old Latin author gives an account of a woman who believed that she

A powerful woman.
"could shake all the world with her finger," and was afraid to close her hand, lest she should crush it like an apple. So easy the achievement of universal reformation seemed to be that the obvious reason for delaying it was the same that restrained the powerful woman, — a merciful hesitation of power, — a shuddering dread of disturbing things. Ah! the omnipotence of edict, fiat, decree, ukase, act of parliament, act of congress, act of assembly, ordinance of council! I did not then know of the

Dead statutes.
countless statutes that are inoperative or dead from indisposition or inability to enforce them. What suggestive great books could be made by collecting them!— mock-

ing commentaries upon the conceit and im-
potence of statesmanship.   My scheme for *His scheme*
delivering the world from evil was for the
reformed of every place to assemble themselves together ;— those

who never drink ;

who use no pernicious drugs ;

who never gorge themselves at table ;

who are never concupiscent ;

who are never unchaste in thought, lan-
    guage, or conduct ;

who perfectly control their appetites and
    passions ;

who never deceive ;

who never lie, prevaricate, or conceal the *The good.*
    truth ;

who do not love money ;

who do not oppress or insult the poor ;

who do not envy or impugn the rich ;

who do no wrong thing ;—

to take into consideration the miserable
multitude,

who do drink ;

who do make use of deleterious drugs ;

who do overtax their digestive powers ;

who are now and then concupiscent ;   *The bad.*

who are sometimes unchaste in thought,
    language, and conduct ;

who do not control their desires and appe-
    tites ;

who deceive;

Those who lie, etc.

who lie, prevaricate, and conceal the truth;

who underestimate and grind the poor;

who love money;

who envy the rich, and impugn their motives and conduct;

who do many wrong things; —

and at once, then and there, devise irrefragable prohibitory laws for the absolute and complete reformation of their imperfect brethren.

The good to convert the bad, and kill the devil.

To prohibit was to prohibit. An exceeding great army to kill the devil. The earth to be made a paradise again. But the world got in and possessed me before the great scheme was announced. My opportunity was lost, and things have gone on in the usual bad way. Can it be, at last, that reforming is much a personal matter, to each one of us? Each to "cease to do evil, and learn to do well." It would seem so.

The agony I suffered all of last night! I believe it is the gout. The doctor doesn't think so; but doctors differ. "If your

A saying of Montaigne.

physician," says Montaigne, "does not think it good for you to sleep, to drink wine, or to eat such and such meats, never trouble yourself; I will find you another

that shall not be of his opinion." He calls
it acute rheumatism, and says I read too
much ! As if that had anything to do
with gout ! Though I do admit the close
relation of mind and body, and know how *Mind and body.*
curiously they sometimes affect each other.
I mean to make a study of their interde-
pendence, and know more of it. But how
a few hours of study in my library could
produce a fit of the gout is incomprehen-
sible to me. From whatever cause, it
is here, and must be removed. My limb
in a vise, with two giants twisting it,
would not be more horrible than the agony I suffer. The Duke of Northumberland suffered from gout. He had tried, he
said, every remedy for it, as he believed,
except one, which, in the case of a friend
of his, proved efficacious, viz., the basti- *The basti-*
nado. This had been applied to his friend *nado for gout.*
when traveling in Turkey, who was dis-
abled by gout from descending from his
palanquin to pay the required homage to
the Grand Vizier ; and it actually cured
him ! I trust so fearful a remedy may not
be necessary in my case.

I feel, and watch, and count my pulsa- *Counts his pulsations.*
tions by the hour sometimes   George

Washington died watching his pulse, and I believe I shall do the same. Haller *Haller did the same.* kept feeling his pulse to the last moment, and when he found that life was almost gone, he turned to his brother physician, observing, " My friend, the artery ceases to beat," and almost instantly expired. The same remarkable circumstance had *And Harvey.* occurred to the great Harvey; he kept making observations on the state of his pulse when life was drawing to its close ; " as if," as was said, "that he who had taught us the beginning of life, might himself, at his departing from it, become acquainted with that of death." Everything I know about the circulation terrifies me. *The heart a wonderful thing.* The heart — what a wonderful thing it is ! To it we refer our joys, our sorrows, and our affections ; yet when grasped with the fingers, it gives no information of the fact to the possessor, unmistakably responding at the same time to the varied emotions of the mind. I think of these mysteries, in hours of sleeplessness, till I am almost distracted. *Accidents and contingencies.* Then the accidents and contingencies of life appear to vex me. A thousand of them, it seems to me, appear to my mind at the same time. Though happenings, I try to think they are not always misfortunes. There was that remarkable *Dinner at Barrère's.* dinner, one hot day, at Barrère's — mentioned by Carlyle in his History. At this dinner, the day being so hot, the guests all stript their coats, and left them in the drawing-room: whereupon Carnot glided out; groped in Robespierre's pocket; found a list of forty [to be butchered by the guillotine], his own name among them; "and tarried not at the wine-cup that day!" At that fearful time, human life was nothing, and human bodies were treated as brutes. At Meudon, says Montgaillard, there was a tannery of human skins; such *A tannery of human skins.* of the guillotined as seemed worth flaying: of which perfectly good wash-leather was made; for breeches and other uses. The skin of the men, he remarks, was superior in toughness and quality to chamois; that of the women was good for almost nothing, being so soft in texture. Which reminds me that after the battle of Munda, on the Guadalquivir, near Cordova, where Cæsar routed the Pompeians, Munda (says Froude in his life of Cæsar) was at once blockaded, the inclosing wall *A wall built of dead bodies.* — savage evidence of the temper of the conquerors — being built of dead bodies pinned together with lances, and on the top of it a fringe of heads on sword's points with the faces turned towards the town.

A man and a woman called to know if I was supplied with the Bible! There was nothing about them to remind me of "the shepherd" and "the mother-in-law" in Pickwick. Oh, no! Though I did detect a degree of self-righteousness lurking in their countenances. I might have shown them our Bible in every English version, and the bible of the Hindoos, of the Parsees, of the Mahometans, and of the Mormons. Respectfully they retired. I did not remark the least condescension. The woman had, I thought, somewhat the look of old grandmother Falconer, who was a terror to her neighborhood; because, being a law to herself, she would therefore be a law to other people. The healthy heart that said to itself, "How healthy am I!" was already fallen into the fatalest sort of disease. Is not sentimentalism (I am quoting Carlyle) twin sister to cant, if not one and the same with it? Is not cant the materia prima of the devil; from which all falsehoods, imbecilities, abominations body them-

Self-right-eousness.

Sentimen-talism and cant.

selves ; from which no two things can
come ? For cant is itself properly a dou-
ble-distilled lie ; the second power of a
lie. The brain (says Dean Swift), in its *Quotes Swift.*
natural position and state of serenity, dis-
poseth its owner to pass his life in the
common forms without any thought of
subduing multitudes to his own power, his
reasons, or his visions ; and the more he
shapes his understanding by the pattern of
human learning, the less he is inclined to
form parties after his particular notions ;
because that instructs him in his private
infirmities, as well as in the stubborn ignorance of the people. But when a man's
fancy gets astride on his reason ; when
imagination is at cuffs with the senses ; *Imagination at cuffs with the senses.*
and common understanding, as well as
common sense, is kicked out of doors, the
first proselyte he makes is himself ; and
when that is once compassed, the difficulty
is not so great in bringing over others ; a
strong delusion always operating from
without, as vigorously as from within. For
cant and vision are to the ear and the eye
the same that tickling is to the touch.
Those entertainments and pleasures we *The entertainments and pleasures we most value.*
most value in life are such as dupe and
play the wag with the senses. For, if we

take an examination of what is generally understood by happiness, as it has respect either to the understanding or the senses, we shall find all its properties and adjuncts will herd under this short definition : that it is a perpetual possession of being well deceived. Thomas Hood, of all men, had the greatest detestation of canters. An awful widow, it is stated, having long pestered him with her insolent tracts and impious admonitions, he at length turned upon her, and wrote her a letter, — his Tract, as he styled it, — in which, perhaps, he used language somewhat too violent. He seems to have thought so himself, and concluded his performance with an apology. "And now, madam, farewell. Your mode of recalling yourself to my memory reminds me that your fanatical mother insulted mine in the last days of her life (which was marked by every Christian virtue) by the presentation of a Tract addressed to Infidels. I remember also that the same heartless woman intruded herself, with less reverence than a Mohawk squaw would have exhibited, on the chamber of death, and interrupted with her jargon almost my very last interview with my dying parent. Such reminiscences war-

Hood's detestation of canters.

Less reverential than a Mohawk squaw.

rant some severity; but if more be want-
ing, know that my poor sister has been
excited by a circle of canters like yourself
into a religious frenzy, and is at this moment in a private mad-house." Goodness, *Goodness*
says Lamb, blows no trumpet, nor desires *blows no*
trumpet.
to have any blown. "How beautiful, great,
and pure goodness is! It paints heaven
on the face that has it; it wakens the
sleeping souls that meet it." "The throne
of the gods is on the brow of a righteous
man." Alas! the devil lurks in many
faces. The Arabs tell a thousand stories
of certain hot waters in a grotto, which
they call Pharaoh's Bath; among others, *Pharaoh's*
Bath.
that if you put four eggs in it, you can
take out but three, the devil always keeping one for himself. Innocence, unmitigated, is with the angels in heaven, and in
pure little children on earth. "You wished
to see Adam and Eve, who were our first
parents; there they are;" said the dau-
phine to her children. Then she left them
in great astonishment before Titian's pic- *Titian's*
picture.
ture, and seated herself by the bedside of
the king, who delighted to watch the children. "Which of the two is Adam?"
said Francis, nudging his sister Margaret's
elbow. "You silly," replied she; "to know

that, they would have to be dressed." Said a sweet little boy, five years old, to his mother, "Which am I, a boy or a girl? I forget." Pretty incidents like these, in contrast with the ugly philanthropy that invaded my quiet with its self-righteous-

A signif-icant Hin-doo fable.

ness, recalls the significant Hindoo fable : Vishnu spake, "O Bal! take thy choice; with five wise men shalt thou enter hell, or with five fools pass into paradise." Gladly answered Bal, "Give me, O Lord, hell with the wise; for that is heaven where the wise dwell, and folly would make of heaven itself a hell!"

A visit from his cousin Tom.

Cousin Tom, whom I have not seen for forty years, came unexpectedly to spend a few days with me. He has, to say the least, interested me very much. He is one of those persons they call professional invalids. The first words he said after his arrival were words of complaint. The great, lusty fellow came steaming in, com-plaining of the cold, when the mercury was only about twenty degrees above zero. I was glad to see him, and glad to have an

An interest-ing charac-ter.

opportunity of studying such an interest-ing character. Tidings of him had reached me from time to time through letters from

my aunt Jane, — who always mentioned
him kindly, but with slight expression of
inextinguishable disgust at some of his
ways. He troubles everybody about him
with his perpetual complaints, but never *Always complaining.*
in his life was he seriously sick. He
weighs two hundred pounds, and is as
round-limbed and muscular as he was at
twenty. His teeth are all sound, and
shine like ivory. " Sovereignty would
have pawned her jewels for them." A
marvel of health, he is ever repeating the
litany of his little miseries. To see him
eat, and then to hear him complain of his
digestion ! He clears voraciously his
plate, piled up heaping with the richest
viands, and then laments that he is not an *Laments that he is not*
anaconda ! It makes a sick man ashamed *an anaconda.*
to see a well man such a fool. Nothing
in the world is the matter with him but
crop-sickness — the disgusting result of
habitual over-feeding. His cough, that he
has been dying of for twenty years, is of
the stomach, sheerly and unmistakably.
He feeds excessively, and suffers some-
what, of course — why not ? Is the man's *His head of*
head of no use to him ? Else, why persist *no use to him.*
in his folly ? Is there, to think of it, anything so common that is of so little use as

heads? The eggs and the sausages that
the man ate for breakfast yesterday, and
the cups of strong coffee that he drank to
hasten them down! And then to hear

Swears at his diges-tion, and en-vies the healthy. him swear at his digestion, and envy the
healthy! I had to endure it all, though
suffering at the time most acutely from an
abscess, or rupture, or something, that is
threatening my life. While he was moan-
ing and groaning over his slight uneasi-
nesses — the result of his enormous indulgence and intemperance — I could n't help
wishing that he could be really sick awhile,
to know what real sickness is, and be cured
of his pretenses. Later in the day his

Scolds his nerves. abused nerves came in for a share of scolding, when he had devoured and burned to-
bacco enough to poison a peccary. But
why lecture him about his disgusting appetites? The stomach has no ears. Self-
command does n't come of preaching — it
is a result of self-training, self-denial, and

Madame de Genlis. endurance. Madame de Genlis was born
with numberless little antipathies; she
had a horror of all insects, particularly of
spiders and frogs. She was also afraid of
mice, and her father made her feed and
bring up one. He obliged her to catch
spiders with her fingers, and to hold toads

in her hands. At such times, though she felt that the blood had forsaken her veins, she was forced to obey. And so a habit *The habit of self-com-* of self-command was established in the *mand.* woman who afterward became so commanding in the French capital and at the court of France. Lamenting and wishing in such a case would have done no good, while discipline accomplished so much. Says Saadi : —

" Had the cat wings, no sparrow could live in the air;   *A verse* Had each his wish, what more would Allah have to *from Saadi.* spare ? "

If some such a result attended my cousin's indulgence as the story illustrates, there would be some compensation in it. It is of a workman pulling his wife out of a ditch, with the remark, " Why, Nanny, you are drunk." " And what do that argify, if I am happy ? " Charles Mathews, *One of Charles* in one of his amusing entertainments, used *Mathews'* to tell a story of a certain innkeeper, who *stories.* made it a rule of his house, to allow a candle to a guest only on condition of his ordering a pint of wine. Whereupon the guest contends, on the reciprocity system, for a light for every half-bottle, and finally drinks himself into a general illumination. But the belly-gods get no pleasure from their indulgence except while they are eating. They are hardly away from the table, when they begin to complain of their aches. It is a wonder that they don't get provoked at their own growling. Crabb Robinson refers to the continued barking of a dog, irritated by the echo of his own voice, which was made by Wordsworth the subject of a sonnet. In human life this is constantly occurring. It is said that a dog has been known to contract an illness by the continued labor of barking at his own echo. My cousin Tom is invariably seized with a fit of coughing whenever a cough is recollected, referred to, or heard. A remembrance of his own pretended ailment is sure to be followed by a violent, sonorous expiration. It is a wonder that his whole breathing and swallowing apparatus was not long ago torn to pieces by his persistent straining ; and not a bit surprising that something like an asthma should have crept into his chest — the direct result, not so much of his stomach cough, as the habit of indulging and cultivating it. Attending to his cough has been a great part of his business for twenty years — a transparent excuse for his chronic idleness. If he had had to earn each one of his dollars

Crabb Robinson of a barking dog.

Cousin Tom's fit of coughing.

His cough an excuse for idleness.

by ten hours in the sun, his cough, as he
calls it, would never have existed. Occu- *Occupation*
pation is the great blessing; we must be *the great blessing*
engaged at something or suffer. Diana
was chaste because she was never idle, but
always busy about her hunting. But for
every day's diligence in my library I do
believe I should not myself be able to survive. Nothing but my books could enable
me to endure my distresses. There is a
story of a gentleman who was under close
confinement in the Bastile seven years; *A story of*
during which time he amused himself with *the Bastile.*
scattering a few small pins about his
chamber, gathering them up again, and
placing them in different figures on the
arm of a great chair. He often told his
friends afterwards that unless he had
found out this piece of employment, he
verily believed he should have lost his
senses. Sir Astley Cooper, when in re- *Sir Astley*
tirement, satiated with wealth and honors, *Cooper.*
is described as looking over the trees of
his park with a conviction that some day
he should hang himself from one of them.
He had spent his life in routine work, and
it was too late to educate his mind to anything else. Ennui, as Madame Roland de-
fines it, is the disease of hearts without

feeling, and of minds without resources. A writer in the London Spectator calls it a mental low fever. It has also been defined to be an afflicting sensation for want of a sensation. Whatever it is, idleness is the prime cause of it. Montaigne relates that when once walking in the fields he was accosted by a beggar of Herculean frame, who solicited alms. "Are you not ashamed to beg?" said the philosopher, with a frown, — "you who are so palpably able to work?" "Oh, sir," was the sturdy knave's drawling rejoinder, "if you only knew how lazy I am!" Jeremy Taylor said to a lady of his acquaintance, who had been very neglectful of the education of her son, "Madam, if you do not choose to fill your boy's head with something, believe me, the devil will." The Turks have a proverb that the devil tempts all other men, but that idle men tempt the devil. In general, says Montesquieu, we place idleness among the beatitudes of heaven; it should rather be put among the torments of hell.

For one, I believe and affirm that the idle, self-indulgent, professional invalid ought to be put out of the way. He de-

Idleness the cause of ennui.

Jeremy Taylor's reply.

The professional invalid.

presses and irritates and aggravates and
infuriates everybody who is much with
him or about him. The atmosphere he
carries with him is blighting. The infi-
nite ill effects of permitting him to live is *Effects of permitting him to live illustrated.*
illustrated in the results of the mistaken
humanity of the philosopher in his treatment of the flea, described so felicitously
by a veracious Frenchman. Causes and
effects are set down numerically. I. The
former, having been bitten by the latter,
seized and was about to dispatch his foe,
when he reflected that the little insect had
only acted from instinct, and was not to
be blamed. Accordingly, he deposited the
flea on the back of a passing dog. II. This
dog was the poodle of a lady, and she was *The poodle of a lady.*
very fond of the pretty animal. On his
return to the house, his mistress took him
upon her lap to caress him, and the flea
embraced the opportunity to change his
habitat. III. The flea having in the course
of the night engaged in active business
operations, awakened the lady. Her husband was sleeping peacefully beside her,
and in the silence of the chamber she
heard him in his dreams whisper, with an *Jealousy aroused*
access of ineffable tenderness, a name!
The name was that of her most intimate

friend.   IV. As soon as it was day the outraged wife hurried to the house of her rival, and told the rival's husband of the big damning discovery she had made.   He, being a man of decision, at once called out the destroyer of his household's peace, and ran him through.   V. The widow, when her husband was taken home to her on a shutter, was so terribly smitten with remorse that she precipitated herself from the fourth story window.   VI. The other lady convinced her husband that he had wronged her by entertaining any suspicion as to her fidelity, and, becoming reconciled with him, seized an early opportunity of poisoning him.   VII. Inasmuch as the jurors of that country had never heard of "extenuating circumstances," and the Chief Magistrate, thinking that he could not put a murderer to better uses than by guillotining him, the guilty woman was duly beheaded, and the sole survivors of the tragedy were the philosopher and the flea.   It would not do to provide hospitals for the professional invalids.   The effect of herding them would be much the same as that resulting from the habit of old Jews from all parts of the world, who go to lay their bones upon the sacred soil (described so

The big damning discovery.

Reconciled.

The sole survivors the philosopher and the flea.

vividly by Kinglake in his matchless little
book of travel). "As these people," he
says, " never return to their homes, it fol-
lows that any domestic vermin which they
may bring with them are likely to become
permanently resident, so that the population is continually increasing. No recent
census had been taken when I was at Tibe-
rias, but I know that the congregation of
fleas which attended at my church alone
[what could be more remindful of the
numberless irritating effects of voluntary
invalidism?] must have been something
enormous. It was a carnal, self-seeking
congregation, wholly inattentive to the
service which was going on, and devoted
to the one object of having my blood.
The fleas of all nations were there. The
smug, steady, importunate flea from Holy-
well street — the pert, jumping, 'puce'
from hungry France — the wary, watch-
ful 'pulce' with his poisoned stiletto —
the vengeful ' pulga ' of Castile with his
ugly knife — the German 'floh' with his
knife and fork — insatiate — not rising
from table — whole swarms from all the
Russias, and Asiatic hordes unnumbered
—all these were there, and all rejoiced in
one great international feast. After pass-

A suggestive passage from King-lake.

A carnal, self-seeking congrega-tion.

Swarms and hordes.

ing a night like this [bad enough, but not to be compared with three whole days with Tom], you are glad to pick up the wretched remains of your body long, long before morning dawns. Your skin is scorched — your temples throb; your lips feel withered and dried; your burning eyeballs are screwed inwards against the brain. You have no hope but only in the saddle, and in the freshness of the morning air." Unhappily, these miserable professional invalids that I am writing about and illustrating constitute a privileged class of society. Charles Lamb called them "kings." Such persons, whether their imagined diseases be of the mind or body, in the opinion of the dissecting Hawthorne, are made acutely conscious of a self, by the torture in which it dwells. Self, therefore, grows to be so prominent an object with them, that they cannot but present it to the face of every carnal passer-by. This cousin of mine is so wrapped up in himself — is such a sublime egotist — that when I mention a real distress of my own — that threatens life itself with its awful gravity — he gives but a lazy, half-attention — amounting to no more, at best, than what Coleridge calls a mental yawn. To have

Glad to pick up the remains of your body.

Professional invalids a privileged class.

Totally selfish.

one's ills aggravated in that manner by a
mere pretender in misery is enough to
awaken all the Satanic in human nature.
I wish my cousin would go away. Even *Wishes his*
cousin would
sick people, I think, with Montaigne (who *go away.*
was much of an invalid himself, and talked
quite enough of his maladies), should publish and communicate their joy, as much
as they can, and conceal and smother their
grief. He that makes himself pitied without reason is a man not to be pitied when
there shall be real cause ; to be always
complaining is the way never to get sympathy ; by making himself out always so
miserable, he is never commiserated by *Never com-*
any. He that makes himself dead when *miserated.*
living is subject to be held as though
alive when he is dying. "We are apt,"
says Hawthorne again, "to make sickly
people more morbid, and unfortunate people more miserable, by endeavoring to
adapt our deportment to their especial and
individual needs. They eagerly accept
our well-meant efforts ; but it is like returning their own sick breath back upon
themselves, to be breathed over and over
again, intensifying the inward mischief at
every repetition. The sympathy that *The sympa-*
thy that
would really do them good is of a kind *would do*
them good.

that recognizes their sound and healthy
parts, and ignores the part affected by disease, which will thrive under the eye of a
too close observer like a poisonous weed
in the sunshine." Herodotus speaks of a
tribe who treated their sick in a way pe-
Discourag- culiarly discouraging to invalidism. When
*ing to in-
validism.* any one fell sick, his chief friends told
him that the illness would spoil his flesh ;
whereupon he would protest that he was
not unwell ; but they, not agreeing with
him, would kill and eat him. Naturalists
A habit of tell us that if one of a flock of wolves
wolves. wound himself, or so much as limp, the
rest eat him up incontinently. Oh ! Mercy
on me ! Three days more of my cousin
Tom would kill me. Will he never go
away ?

In rearranging my books this morning I
encountered a favorite volume that I had
missed the sight of for a year or two. I
was glad to see it — a valuable old friend.
Foster's Es- It is a little, rude copy in boards of Foster's
says. Essays — Andover, 1826. This is one of
those little books that have had incalculable
influence. It is filled with vigorous, cast-
iron thought, from the first word to the last.
The author often spent hours on a single

sentence. I know of nothing in literature
that is a better stimulant for the mind, or
tonic for the character, than the essay on
Decision. And, strange to say, these es-
says were written as love epistles to the *Written as love epistles.*
lady who afterward became his wife. She
had intimated to him that she could never
consent to be the wife of a man who could
not distinguish himself in the literature of
his country; and the famous essays were
written to her in the form of letters, to
prove to her that he possessed the requisite
ability. Miss Maria Snooke, I think, was *Miss Maria Snooke.*
the name of the notably exacting maiden.
She must have been a remarkable woman.
He describes her in his Diary (at the time
he was courting her) as "a marble statue,
surrounded by iron palisades." Long ago,
when I was a bit of a boy, I saw it stated
that a distinguished American orator and
statesman, then living, had said that he
owed incomparably more to Foster's Essays than to any other one book in literature. Remembering the statement, I tried
again and again to buy the book; but the *Efforts to buy the book.*
bookseller knew nothing about it. At last,
I found it in a gentleman's library, offered
for sale in pecuniary extremity; he being
one of those rare individuals who could be

economical in everything but in books. It was put up by the auctioneer only a minute after I had dropped in, and I was so delighted at the prospect of being the owner of the long-sought volume, that I bid three quarters of a dollar for it at once, and it was as quickly knocked down to me, — the gaping bystanders, of course, laughing heartily at me for giving so much for a little half-worn book that I might as well have had for a shilling. I went home elated with my purchase, and spent half the night over it. It was very evident that its former owner was an intelligent and close reader, for some very significant marks and reflections covered the margins of some of the pages. Wherever I went, I always carried the treasure with me ; and later, it was one of the few books I always kept in my downtown office. It was one of the most comfortable offices in the block, and two or three of the dozen women employed by the janitor, by permission, enjoyed its comforts on Sundays and at odd hours when I was absent. One of them was a remarkable person, and I have often thought of her since. Margaret, I remember, was the girl's name. She must have had the blood of kings in her veins. Of the books on the shelf, she

Knocked down to him.

The treasure.

Margaret.

liked Foster's Essays best, she said ; of
which both the appearance of the volume
and her acquaintance with it gave indubita-
ble evidence. She had a very strong mind
and magnificent passions. There was majesty in her mien, though a poor working wo-
man. Regal she was, in countenance, sug- *Regal in countenance.*
gesting Zenobia or Cleopatra. She seemed
to me to be "clad in the usual weeds of
high habitual state," so commanding and
noble was her bearing. Her hair was so
abundant as to appear a burden to her.
But her remarkable eye is most distinct in
my memory. It was a true Irish eye, —
"gray, with long, dark lashes, and with lids
deep set and well chiseled, — an eye speaking mingled innocence, mirth, and tenderness quite unmatched by any human orb."
Once I saw it when it seemed to hover and
melt over the dear spot and dear ones in
her far-away, never-forgotten home, on the
other side of the sea. Moore's pen would
have run wild describing her. But the
black drop was somehow mingled in her *The black drop in her nature.*
rich nature. "The beautiful river ! The
beautiful river !" she exclaimed, looking
down out of the fourth story window, with
that pensive far-away expression so peculiar to her; and a moment after she was

picked up in the court, a pitiful, quivering mass of dead humanity. At the inquest I had an opportunity of paying tribute to her strong understanding and lofty moral nature. I set this down at a time when every faculty of my mind seems floating in reminiscence.

The perfect ballad. It takes two at least, it seems, to make a perfect ballad. "What can be prettier," says Cowper, in one of his exquisite letters, "than Gay's ballad, or rather Swift's, Arbuthnot's, Pope's, and Gay's, in the What do you call it?—''T was when the seas were roaring'? I have been well informed that that most celebrated association of clever fellows all contributed to it." And I suspect Gay had like help in the composition of Black Eyed Susan — another of his ballads not less remarkable for its perfection. *John Anderson, my jo, John.* John Anderson, my jo, John, all the world has been in the habit of regarding as another perfect ballad, till a verse lately added to it by a gentleman in northern Ohio proved it to have been, as Burns left it, far from being perfect. The additional verse was sent to me in manuscript, as taken from the lips of the author, and should make his name famous if he never wrote another line. I have copied it into the margin of my Burns, alongside the poem, and also copy it here, to preserve it further, in case the book should be spirited away.

> "John Anderson, my jo, John,
> We winna mind that sleep;
> The grave sae cauld and still, John,
> The spirit canna keep:
> But we will wake in Heaven, John,
> Where young again we 'll grow,
> And ever live, in blessèd luve,
> John Anderson, my jo."

An additional verse

How Burns and the author of this stanza will strike hands on the other shore! I should like to witness the meeting of the two bards. Ah! the matchless poet of humanity! "Since Adam," said Margaret Fuller, "there has been none that approached nearer fitness to stand up before God and angels in the naked majesty of manhood than Robert Burns." But she *Burns.* speaks of the "serpent in his field also." Though two nieces of Burns, living in the suburbs of Ayr, believed, when talked to by an American lady about Burns' intemperate habits, that they had been greatly exaggerated. Their mother was a woman twenty-five years old and the mother of three children when he died, and she had never once seen him the "waur for liquor."

"There were very many idle people i' the warld, an' a great deal o' talk," they said.

Byron's question. "What," asks Byron, in his Journal, "would Burns have been, if a patrician? We should have had more polish — less force — just as much verse, but no immortality — a divorce, and a duel or two, the which had he survived, as his potations must have been less spirituous, he might *A reference to Sheridan.* have lived as long as Sheridan, and outlived as much as poor Brinsley." Of Scotland, it has been significantly remarked, the creed is the Westminster Confession, but the national poet is Burns.

It is Saint Valentine's Day, and there is *A dance at the house opposite.* a dance at the house opposite. I can just see, through the lace curtains, the "floating radiances" swimming and gliding about. How it all carries me back! Ah! at twenty, with a sweetheart of sixteen! Happy then, miserable now. At the recollection, my heart "flows like a sea." It is the touch of a maiden's hand, according to the Oriental legend, that causes the trees to bloom. "For the first time," says Jean Paul, "I held a beloved being upon my heart and *The one pearl of a minute.* lips. I have nothing further to say, but that it was the one pearl of a minute, that was never repeated ; a whole longing past and a dreaming future were united in a moment, and in the darkness behind my closed eyes the fire-works of a whole life were evolved in a glance. Ah, I have never forgotten it — the ineffaceable moment ! " Madame *Madame Roland.* Roland, at sixteen, is described as most fascinating in mind and person. Many suitors began to appear, one after another, but she manifested no interest in any of them. The customs of society in France were such at that time, that it was difficult for any one who sought the hand of the young lady to obtain an introduction to her. Consequently the expedient was usually adopted of writing first to her parents. These letters were always immediately shown to her. She judged of the character of the writer by the character of the epistles. Her father, knowing her intellectual superiority, looked to her as his secretary to reply to all *Her father's secretary in* these letters. She consequently wrote the *delicate matters.* answers, which her father carefully copied and sent in his own name. She was often amused with the gravity with which she, as the father of herself, with parental prudence, discussed her own interests. In subsequent years she wrote to kings and to cabinets in the name of her husband ;

and the sentiments which flowed from her pen, adopted by the ministry of France as

Guided the councils of nations.

their own, guided the councils of nations. Beauty is in the eye of the gazer, and is beauty still, however you disguise it. The Duc de Richelieu had a portrait gallery of contemporary beauties, each attired in the costume of a nun. The magic of the ten-

Lamartine's passionate love-story.

der passion! Raphael, in Lamartine's passionate love-story, regarded his Julie as one of those delusions of fancy, one of those women above mortal height, like Tasso's Eleonora, Dante's Beatrice, Petrarch's Laura, or Vittoria Colonna, the lover, the poet, and the heroine at once; forms that flit across the earth, scarcely touching it, and without tarrying, only to fascinate the eyes of some men, the privileged few of love, to lead on their souls to immortal aspirations, and to be the sursum corda of superior im-

Disillusion.

aginations. But the disillusion, after being wrought up by the dazzling contemplation! An old book of English legal reminiscences tells us that on the Norfolk circuit the famous Jack Lee was retained for the plaintiff in an action for breach of promise of marriage: when the brief was brought him, he asked whether the lady for whose injury he was to seek redress was good-looking.

" Very handsome, indeed, sir," was the assurance of Helen's attorney. " Then, sir," replied Lee, " I beg you to request her to be in court, and in a place where she can be seen." The attorney promised compliance ; and the lady, in accordance with Lee's wishes, took her seat in a conspicuous place. Lee, in addressing the jury, did not fail to insist with great warmth on the "abominable cruelty" which had been practiced towards "the lovely and confiding female" before them, and did not sit down until he had succeeded in working up their feelings to the desired point. The counsel on the other side, however, speedily broke the spell with which Lee had enchanted the jury, by observing that his learned friend in describing the graces and beauty of the plaintiff had not mentioned the fact — that the lady had a wooden leg! The court was convulsed with laughter, while Lee, who was ignorant of this circumstance, looked aghast ; and the jury, ashamed of the influence that mere eloquence had had upon them, returned a verdict for the defendant. "Ah, poor Pen !" exclaims Thackeray, when Pen was no longer in love with the Fotheringay, " the delusion is better than the truth sometimes, and fine dreams to dismal waking." Though, happen what may, we will recur to the good times agone, and con-

sole ourselves in the philosophic manner of the same great master : " I am," he says, " tranquil : I am quiet : I have passed the hot stage : and I do not know a pleasanter and calmer feeling of mind than that of a respectable person of the middle age, who

can still be heartily and generously fond of all the women about whom he was in a passion and a fever in early life. If you cease liking a woman when you cease loving her, depend on it, that one of you is a bad one. You are parted, never mind with what pangs on either side, or by what circumstances of fate, choice, or necessity, — you have no money or she has too much, or she likes somebody else better, and so forth ; but an honest Fogy should always,

unless reason be given to the contrary, think well of the woman whom he has once thought well of, and remember her with kindness and tenderness, as a man remembers a place where he has been very happy." But the dance at the house opposite. The movement seems to me too rapid. There is not enough of repose, so to speak, in the modern dancing. I should like once more to see a minuet, in the old-time style.

The minuet was the dance of kings, the poetry of the courtly salon. George Washington was at home in the stately movement, and he has been pronounced "the most decorous and respectable person that ever went ceremoniously through the realities of life." Hawthorne imagined he was born with his clothes on, and his hair powdered, and made a stately bow on his first appearance in the world. I should like to set down the circumstance of Gouverneur Morris's rebuff, upon approaching familiarly the great American idol — related so inter- estingly by an early annalist ; but my hand is weary with too much writing. The doctor will scold. I can only refer to the contrast of the ancient, reposeful minuet, with the unceremonious, rapid, familiar waltz of the moderns, and quote some piquant lines, inclosed by Sir Thomas Lawrence to Lord Mountjoy : —

ON WALTZING.

" What ! the girl I adore by another embraced !
What ! the balm of her breath shall another man taste !
What ! pressed in the whirl by another's bold knee !
What ! panting, recline on another than me !
Sir, she 's yours. You have brushed from the grape its
    soft blue ;
From the rosebud you 've shaken its tremulous dew :
What you 've touched you may take — pretty waltzer
    adieu ! "

Books.   My books! What would my life be without them? They are my meat and my drink. They employ my mind and lift me out of myself. In hours of mental exaltation I forget my miserable body. I have a book for every mood and every condition. When my mind is strongest and clearest and freest, I range the upper fields of phi-

Plato.   losophy with Plato; when I am most inclined to pure reason, I listen to brave Socrates; when I am in temper for observation, I read Æsop; when I want to realize the power of light over darkness, I tread the dawn with Epictetus; when I want to breathe the atmosphere of the Cæsars, I follow Suetonius; then I walk with Cicero and his nomenclator in the streets of the Eternal City, and study the arts of the Roman politician; of moral exaltation, I find a rare example in the heathen em-

Marcus Antoninus.   peror Marcus Antoninus; gods, and demigods, and heroes fight for me in Homer; if I want to sup with horrors, I sit down in terror with Æschylus, witnessing the ghost of Clytemnestra rushing into Apollo's temple, and rousing the sleeping Furies; if I want a refreshing ride in the chariot of the sun, I take a seat with Phaëton, in Ovid; at will, I range paradise with Mil-

ton, and explore perdition with Dante;
when I hunger for the world, and want to
see every type of man and woman perfectly represented, I read Shakespeare; *Shake-*
when I want to study human nature, I *speare.*
take Don Quixote, Pilgrim's Progress, and
Faust; to feel the inspiration of freedom,
I scale the heights and storm the fast-
nesses with Schiller; I gossip with wise
old Montaigne; think with Pascal; moral- *Montaigne.*
ize with Sir Thomas Browne; quote and
comment with Burton; rummage with Disraeli; laugh with Rabelais; enjoy the suggestive experiences of Gil Blas; am always
amused and entertained with Tristram
Shandy; Tom Jones — who could ever tire
of it? or of Humphry Clinker? or of Rod-
erick Random? or Swift's Gulliver? though
I am terrified sometimes with its pitiless
wisdom; I go a-fishing with Izaak, and *Izaak Wal-*
participate (the slightest) his meekness and *ton.*
sweet contentment; I listen to sermons
from Bourdaloue, and Bossuet, and Massillon, and Barrow, and South, and Chalmers, and Wesley, and Hall; I take down
Foster when I want to read a little and
think more of times gone by and difficulties
overcome; then I philosophize with Souvestre in his Attic; then enjoy the caustic

wit and keen satire of Thackeray, and contemplate his immortal creations ; then the
Dickens. humanities of Dickens quicken me to tears,
and a long procession of the creatures of
his teeming brain move before me ; Sir
Walter, too, who is history enough for me
Burns. now ; and Burns — the one immortal bard
of humanity — to be cherished and sung
while man is man, ever and ever ; and philosophic Wordsworth ; and poetic Shelley
and Keats ; and the moral and wise Sam
Johnson ; and the gentle and exquisite
Goldsmith ; and the storming Carlyle, —
mighty hater and smiter of cant and
shams ; then I discourse with Coleridge ;
pun and turn over rare old books with
Lamb. gentle Elia ; luxuriate with abounding Macaulay ; dream with De Quincey ; expatiate with Hazlitt and Hunt ; then to the
Brontés — Charlotte especially ; then to
Miss Austen — so healthy, serene, and
pure ; then to something more thoughtful
again — to Emerson, the reflective, the
wise, the exalted — fit society for Plato in
the empyrean ; then to Hawthorne — dis-
sector, interpenetrator of hearts and lives ;
to scholarly, witty, shrewd Lowell — critic,
Holmes poet, ambassador ; to Holmes — so acute,
humorous, suggestive, and philosophical in

the Autocrat and Elsie — altogether unique in literature ; and when a taste for something light, and finished, and exquisite, seizes me, I read the Reveries, and Prue and I ; and so I go on and on, feasting with the worthies, and banqueting with the celestials, as inclination or whim pleases me — a precious book, as I said, for every mood and every condition.

Books ! books !   It was estimated, some *Books!* years ago, that ten million volumes, first *books !* and last, had been published since the art of printing was discovered — with an average edition of three hundred — aggregating three thousand million volumes !   Yet tradition in Cambridge has recorded that Bentley said he desired and thought himself likely to live to fourscore, an age long enough, he thought, to read everything which was worth reading.   But single books, and little ones — what influence they have exerted !   Elizabeth Wallbridge, The Dairyman's Daughter, is known to *The Dairy-* every tract distributor in the world.   The *man's* *Daughter.* tract containing the story of her life has been translated into nineteen languages, and has had a circulation of four million copies.   The circulation of Uncle Tom's

Cabin has been even more remarkable.
And Thomas à Kempis's Imitation —
think of the influence of that. Leigh
Hunt, in his Autobiography, speaks of a
riot at Lyons about an equestrian statue of
Louis XIV., meant to overawe the city
with Bourbon memories. We met, he
says, the statue on the road. I had
bought in that city a volume of the songs
of Béranger, and I thought to myself, as I
met the statue, "I have a little book in my
pocket which will not suffer you to last
long." And surely enough, down it went:
for down went King Charles. Books,
thought Mrs. Barbauld, are a kind of perpetual censors on men and manners ; they
judge without partiality, and reprove without fear or affection. There are times
when the flame of virtue and liberty seems
almost to be extinguished amongst the existing generation ; but their animated pages
are always at hand to rekindle it. The
despot trembles on his throne, and the
bold, bad man turns pale in his closet at
the sentence pronounced against him ages
before he was born. Happily, the best
books are the commonest, and are always
in use. Erskine used to say that in addressing juries he had found there were

Béranger.

Animated pages.

three books, and only three, which he could
always quote with effect, Shakespeare, Mil-
ton, and the Bible.   Milton's favorite vol- *Poets' favorites.*
umes were Homer, Ovid, and Euripides ;
Dante's was Virgil ; Schiller's was Shakespeare ; Gray's was Spenser ; Goethe's was
Spinoza's Ethics ; Bunyan's was the old
legend of Sir Bevis of Southampton.   The
two books which most impressed John
Wesley, when young, were the Imitation *Wesley's*
of Christ, and Taylor's Holy Living and *preference.*
Dying.   De Quincey's favorite few were
Donne, Chillingworth, Jeremy Taylor, Milton, South, Barrow, and Sir Thomas
Browne.   Napoleon never wearied of reading Ossian and the Sorrows of Werther.
Miss Austen's novels were favorites with
Macaulay ; he enjoyed them especially for
their serenity.   Thackeray was particularly
fond of Humphry Clinker ; he believed it *Humphry*
to be " the most laughable story that has *Clinker.*
ever been written since the goodly art of
novel-writing began."   Douglas Jerrold had
an almost reverential fondness for books —
books themselves — and said he could not
bear to treat them, or to see them treated,
with disrespect.   It always gave him pain
to see them turned on their faces, stretched
open, or dog's eared, or carelessly flung

down, or in any way misused. Bayle, it is known, gave up every sort of recreation, except that delicious inebriation of his faculties which he drew from his books. If the riches of both Indies, said Fénelon ; if the crowns of all the kingdoms of Europe were laid at my feet, in exchange for my love for reading, I would spurn them all. At this day, said Pope to Spence, as much company as I have kept, and as much as I love it, I love reading better. I would rather be employed in reading than in the most agreeable conversation. There is a story that Dante, having gone one day to the house of a bookseller, from one of whose windows he was to be a spectator of a public show exhibited in the square below, by chance took up a book, in which he soon got so absorbed that on returning home, after the spectacle was over, he solemnly declared that he had neither seen nor heard anything whatever of all that had taken place before his eyes. Scott, in Waverley, describes the Baron of Bradwardine as a scholar, according to the scholarship of Scotchmen ; that is, his learning was more diffuse than accurate, and he was rather a reader than a grammarian. Of his zeal for the classic authors he is said to have given

Delicious inebriation.

Pope to Spence.

Dante absorbed.

Zeal for classic authors.

an unconscious instance. On the road be- *An unconscious instance.*
tween Preston and London he made his
escape from his guards ; but being afterwards found loitering near the place where
they had lodged the former night, he was
recognized and again arrested. His companions, and even his escort, were surprised at his infatuation, and could not
help inquiring why, being once at liberty,
he had not made the best of his way to a
place of safety ; to which he replied, that
he had intended to do so, but, in good
faith, he had returned to seek· his Titus
Livius, which he had forgot in the hurry
of his escape. Plato's cave, in which he *Plato's cave.*
supposes a man to be shut up all his life   .
with his back to the light, and to see nothing of the figures of men or other objects
that pass by but their shadows on the opposite wall of his cell, so that when he is
let out and sees the real figures he is only
dazzled and confounded by them, seemed
to Hazlitt an ingenious satire on the life *Satire on*
of a bookworm. I confess to the French- *the life of a*
man's hatred of a dirty book. It is in *bookworm.*
truth an error to suppose that the dirt on
the cover and pages of a book is a sign of
its studious employment. Those who use
books to most purpose handle them with

Book-bor-rowing. loving care. And as to persistent book-borrowing, book-owners can hardly trust themselves to speak of it. Its commonness does not excuse the offense. It is said that Lord Eldon, when chancellor, greatly augmented his library by borrowing books quoted at the bar; and forgetting to return them, he would say of such borrowers, " Though backward in accounting, they were well-practiced in book-keeping." *Book-thiev-ing.* But deliberate book-thieving — what crime is there to compare with it in the estimation of the student and librarian? In Chambers' Journal there is an account of a memorable literary virtuoso who piqued himself upon his collection of scarce editions and original manuscripts, most of which he had purloined from the libraries of others. He was always borrowing books of acquaintances with a resolution never to return them; sending in a great hurry for a particular edition which he wanted to *Subterfuges.* consult for a moment, but when its return was solicited he was not at home; or he had lent the book to somebody else; or he could not lay his hand upon it just then; or he had lost it; or he had himself already delivered it to the owner. Sometimes he contented himself with stealing

one volume of a set, knowing where to procure the rest for a trifle. After his death
his library was sold at auction, and many
of his defrauded friends had the pleasure
of buying their own property back again *Buying their own property back.*
at an exorbitant price. Reading lately of
book-titles, I was amused with a statement
of how misleading many of them have
been. The Diversions of Purley, at the *Diversions of Purley.*
time of its publication, was ordered by a
village book-club, under the impression
that it was a book of amusing games.
The Essay on Irish Bulls was another
work which was thought by some folks to
deal with live stock. The Ancient Mar-
iner was sold largely to sea-faring men,
who concluded from the name that it had
some relation to nautical matters. The *The Excursion.*
Excursion — expensive copies of it — were
sold to tourists and to keepers of country
inns and boarding-houses, as likely to be
of especial interest to excursionists. James
Smith used to dwell with much pleasure
on the criticism of a Leicestershire clergy-
man : "I do not see why they (the Ad- *Rejected Addresses.*
dresses) should have been rejected : I think
some of them very good." This, he would
add, is almost as good as the avowal of the
Irish bishop, that there were some good

things in Gulliver's Travels which he could not believe. Tocqueville preferred living with books to living with authors. One is not always happy with the latter; while books are intelligent companions, without vanity, ill-humor, or caprice; they do not want to talk of themselves, do not dislike to hear others praised; clever people whom one can summon and dismiss just as one pleases. I often derive a peculiar satisfaction, says Sterne, in conversing with the ancient and modern dead, who yet live and speak excellently in their works. My neighbors think me often alone, and yet at such times I am in company with more than five hundred mutes — each of whom, at my pleasure, communicates his ideas to me by dumb signs, quite as intelligibly as any person living can do by the uttering of words. They always keep the distance from me which I direct, and with a motion of my hand I can bring them as near to me as I please. I lay hands on fifty of them sometimes in an evening, and handle them as I like; they never complain of ill-usage; and when dismissed from my presence, though ever so abruptly, take no offense. How to read? is a grave question to readers. Goethe

*Tocque-
ville's pref-
erence.*

*Sterne's
tribute.*

*How to
read?*

said he had been employed for eighteen years trying to learn the art, and had not attained it. Richter, speaking of miscellaneous reading, inquires, quaintly, "Does more depend on the order in which the meats follow each other or on the digestion of them?" In 1731, Atterbury wrote his last letter to Pope, and asks, "How many books have come out of late in your parts which you think I should be glad to peruse? Name them. The catalogue, I believe, will not cost you much trouble. They must be good ones indeed to challenge any part of my time, now I have so little of it left. I, who squandered whole days heretofore, now husband hours when the glass begins to run low, and care not to spend them on trifles. At the end of the lottery of life our last minutes, like tickets left in the wheel, rise in their valuation." "Marvelous power of mind!" exclaims Souvestre, reflecting on the value of books in old age. "From a corner of my chamber — from the arm-chair which I occupy — I can traverse the immense abysses of the past. I am present at the foundation of cities, the birth and growth of empires; I accompany various races as they wander over the earth, establish them-

Atterbury to Pope.

An exclamation of Souvestre.

Takes note of human- ity. selves, and found nations ; I take note of that perpetual movement of humanity, as it seeks its level on the globe which has been given to it for an inheritance. Or, fatigued with these generalities, I repose in the tent of the patriarch Abraham, or beneath the oak of St. Louis. From the tribune of Cicero I pass to the pulpit of *Distances nothing.* Bossuet ; distances are nothing to me ; I traverse them by an instantaneous bound, whether those of space or time. From the east I hasten to the west, from the early days of the world I pass on to the hour which has just struck ; wherever an at- tractive spectacle summons me, I am there in spirit ; or a noble action or an elevated conversation invites me, I am present to *Magnificent empire of memory !* applaud or take part. Magnificent empire of memory ! vast power and inexhaustible activity of thought ! I cease to be troubled now at my solitude and forced inaction."

A strange dream, or vision. I had a strange dream last night — or vision rather. I record it as a curious freak or exercise of the faculties. The doctor must have put a little too much opium in his last powders. Methought my pretty round table in the library was en- larged to many times its real size. I was

contemplating its polished surface, and
wondering if any wood could be richer and
more beautiful than our American black
walnut, when a pill-box made its appearance on the table, — rolling about in an
erratic way — describing all sorts of circles
and semicircles, in the easiest and most ec-
centric manner possible.   It was a diminutive thing — the tiniest of the kind I had
ever seen — not greater in diameter than
the smallest thimble.   It was so small indeed that a close eye was necessary to observe its movements.   Soon, another pill-
box, a size larger, presented itself, and the
two immediately began chasing each other
in a very amusing manner — sometimes in
straight lines and sometimes in graceful
curves.   Then another pill-box, a size bigger than the last, made its appearance, and
joined with the others in freakish gambols.
A fourth next showed itself — still a little
larger than the third — in a still more rol-
licking humor than any of the rest, and it
became very difficult indeed to watch them,
so rapid and peculiar were their movements.   Then another and another, each
one a little bigger, till the table was pretty
well filled with animated pill-boxes.   There
must have been as many as forty or fifty

A pill-box made its appearance.

The tiniest of its kind.

Still larger.

of them, — of every size and variety, from the minute smallest to that of greatest proportions. No apothecary ever saw a greater array and intermixture. And each was marked with a cabalistic label, such as I had seen many a time in the handwriting of the numerous forgotten doctors my multiplied diseases have baffled. The mysterious characters inscribed on each would have been an interesting study to the archæologist. I wish I had a memorandum of them. The gravest of all my doctors would have laughed at their queerness, their variety, and their multiplicity. Away they all ran — the whole forty or fifty — in infinite variation — describing, it seemed to me, every known figure in geometry, — distinct and in combination. Sometimes I thought their movements described the orbits of the solar system better than any planetarium I had seen. Then in a long curved line they ranged themselves, — the first in the procession being the tiniest, and the last the most gigantic — as big as Gibbon's snuff-box that he tapped so gracefully, and a pinch from which he always let fall at just the right moment to emphasize his story. In that long serpentine line how they did crawl about ; then wrig-

Of every size and variety.

A study for the archæologist.

Every figure in geometry.

Gibbon's snuff-box.

gled and twisted into all sorts of contortions and convolutions; then stretched themselves into something like order again. Their speed was interesting — their revolutions, I mean. The big ones had stately movements, like the great wheels of great engines. There was an expression of power in their slowness, and of apparent contempt for the little bustling fellows that had to be constantly hurrying to keep up. Then they were all mixed up — the little ones and the big ones together. They were so involved that I could not tell one from another; and the wonder was that there was no collision. Then they went leaping and leaping, till it appeared there must be a universal smash. I trembled for the consequences. Then the tops or coverings came off, and mingled miscellaneously with the other parts, showing fresh vigor in the chase, as so many fresh foxes. The boxes that had contained so many incompatibles fused together in close companionship. The opium was not at all disgusted with the lobelia. The jalap and the pleasantest of all soothing remedies affiliated, as if they had been friends since Galen. Then they ranged themselves again into long serpentine lines —

Their revolutions.

Big and little together.

Incompatibles together

the boxes and the lids separate. After al-
ternate slow and rapid movements, they

Playing at leap-frog. began playing at leap-frog — the smallest
being vaulted by the next in size, until the
whole lines were changed — the most diminutive bringing up the rear, and the largest
leading the column. And so they went on
with their varied and indescribable gyra-
tions and convolutions ; when, suddenly
leaping into one another, they nested themselves snugly together ; then as quickly
and mysteriously disappeared, and the remarkable scene was ended. No Roman
emperor in the Flavian amphitheatre was

Dance of the Pill-Boxes. ever better entertained. I call it The
Dance of the Pill-Boxes.

By appointment, the doctor spent a
couple of hours with me last night in my
library. I had anticipated his visit in
every way that I could, and was glad to
see him. The place was cheerfully illumi-
nated, and the wine was the best that my
cellar afforded. I was pleased to see that
he was disposed to be attentive and recep-

Talks of books exclu-sively. tive, as my purpose was to talk to him of
books exclusively, with a view to enlight-
ening him as to some of the best, and to
show him what a comparatively small sum

of money would put him in possession
of them. For, time and again, he has
lamented to me his lack of intelligence on
the subject, as well as of the requisite cash
to buy, even though he knew what books he
should purchase. To convince him that a *To convince the doctor.*
good proportion of the famous books that
have been produced could be put into a
small space, and that not a very large
amount of money would be necessary to
purchase them, I caused two hundred or
more volumes to be placed together in one *Contents of one case.*
case with seven shelves, each of four feet
in length, that he might be convinced by
seeing, as well as by my didactic instruction. To have the whole before us as a
sort of object-lesson, our easy chairs were
so placed that we could view the collection
to the best advantage. The first shelf *The first shelf.*
(the lowest) was just filled with the Bible,
in four volumes (Samuel Bagster & Sons,
London) ; Webster's Unabridged Dictionary ; Anthon's Classical Dictionary ; and
Appleton's Cyclopædia, 16 volumes ; (22
volumes in all). The second shelf was *The second shelf.*
filled with octavos (some of them of two
and more volumes) of Shakespeare, Bacon,
Milton, Homer, Dante, Virgil, Faust,
Chambers' Encyclopædia of English Liter-

ature (London and Edinburgh) ; and Bryant's Library of Poetry and Song. These
Good edi-
tions.
are all good editions, well printed, and appropriately (as I said) in octavo. The
other five shelves contained the following,
— named in the order in which the books
happened to be placed, and not according
to preference. They are in crown octavo,
12mo, and 16mo — a very few of the latter — only such as could not be conven-
iently purchased of a larger size. Plato's
Republic and Phædo, 2 volumes (from
Bohn's Standard Library). Emerson's
A beautiful
edition of
Montaigne.
Prose Works, 2 volumes. Montaigne's
Essays, 4 volumes (the beautiful Riverside
edition — exquisite letter-press — the proof-
sheets of the perfect pages having been
read by Mr. H. O. Houghton himself, long
before he attained the head of the pub-
lishing house of Messrs. Houghton, Mifflin
& Company). Swift's Works, 6 volumes.
Goldsmith's works, 4 volumes. Seneca's
Morals (London, 1702). Carlyle's Essays,
Sartor Resartus, and French Revolution,
6 volumes. Hawthorne's Scarlet Letter
Haw-
thorne's
masterpiece.
(his masterpiece). Holmes's Autocrat, and
Elsie Venner, 2 volumes (the cream of his
genius.) Curtis's Prue and I (a little volume of exquisite sketches). Uncle Tom's

Cabin. Souvestre's Attic Philosopher, and
Leaves from a Family Journal, 2 volumes
(suited to serene moods). De Quincey's
Opium Eater. Sydney Smith (a volume
of selections, including the Peter Plymley
Letters). Wilson's Noctes Ambrosianæ *One volume made up from five.*
(a volume made up from the five original
volumes, containing most that is best and
of general interest). Miss Austen's Pride
and Prejudice. Arabian Nights. Lamb's
Essays, and Talfourd's Life and Letters,
3 volumes. Pascal's Thoughts. Epictetus
(a beautiful edition, Little, Brown & Company). La Rochefoucauld's Maxims (Wil-
liam Gowans, Nassau Street, — that in- *An interesting bibliopolist.*
teresting bibliopolist, known to so many
book-lovers : I could gossip about him for
an hour). Irving's Sketch-Book, Knick-
erbocker's History of New York, and Life
of Goldsmith, 3 volumes (his complete
works would fill a whole shelf). Foster's
Essays. Charlotte Brontë's Jane Eyre.
Mill on Liberty. Gil Blas. Burns (with
marginal glossary, John S. Marr & Sons,
Glasgow, — the most convenient edition *A convenient edition of Burns.*
of Burns for English readers that I know).
Godwin's Caleb Williams. Junius's Letters. Crabb Robinson's Diary. Tragedies
of Æschylus. Butler's Hudibras. Bun-

yan's Pilgrim's Progress. Cicero's Offices,
etc. (a single volume from Bohn's). Holbein's Dance of Death. Macaulay's Essays, 6 volumes. Dana's Two Years Before
the Mast. Darwin's Voyage. Selections
Landor re-
duced
from Savage Landor, by Hillard. (A rich
little book.) Boswell's Johnson, 4 volumes. Burton's Anatomy of Melancholy,
3 volumes. (It would not do to be without
Burton.) Reveries of a Bachelor. (This
Books that
have flavor.
is another of those little books that have
flavor, and must live.) Disraeli's Curiosities of Literature, 4 volumes. Sir Thomas
Browne (Religio Medici, A Letter to a
Friend, Christian Morals, and Urn Burial,
in one attractive volume, imprint, Ticknor
& Fields). Fénelon (a selection from his
writings, Munroe & Company, Boston and
Cambridge). Robinson Crusoe. Wilhelm
Meister. Dickens's Pickwick Papers, Da-
vid Copperfield, and Tale of Two Cities, 3
volumes. (His humor, his pathos, and his
Dickens's
master-
pieces.
power are best displayed in these three
masterpieces.) Letters of Madame de Sévigné. Letters of Lady Mary Wortley Montagu. Rasselas. Walton's Angler.
White's History of Selborne. Thoreau's
Walden. Charles O'Malley. Of the Imitation of Christ. Fielding's Tom Jones

and Humphry Clinker, 2 volumes. Pic-
ciola. Jeremy Taylor's Holy Living and
Holy Dying, 2 volumes. Book of Scottish *A good book of Scottish songs.*
Songs (a volume of the Illustrated London
Library, — an admirable collection, and a
beautiful book). Thomas Fuller's Holy
and Profane States, and Good Thoughts in
Bad Times, 2 volumes (selections from the
works of the old worthy). Confucius, and
the Chinese Classics. Froude's Short
Studies on Great Subjects (the volume con- *Froude's article on the Book of Job.*
taining the article on the Book of Job).
Vanity Fair and The Newcomes. Cooper's
Spy. Balzac's Petty Annoyances of Married Life (one of the most amusing and
acute books in literature, whatever may be
thought of its tone and spirit). Rabelais.
Ecce Homo. (Why has the Professor
never published the promised companion
volume ?) Spence's Anecdotes. Vathek.
Lewis's Monk (a queer, crazy old copy,
printed on different fonts of type, and containing pictures of the veritable devils). Selden's Table Talk. Johnson's Lives of the
English Poets, 2 volumes (to get the Life
of Savage : why don't some publisher print *A suggestion to publishers.*
it separately ?) Aristotle's Ethics. Lu-
ther's Table Talk. Hazlitt's Round Table
volume (containing Conversations of North-

cote). Life of John Brown of Ossawat-
tomie. Montesquieu, 4 volumes. Don
Quixote. Tasso's Jerusalem Delivered.
Kinglake's Eöthen. Jerrold's Mrs. Cau-
dle's Curtain Lectures, and Chronicles of
Clovernook, 2 volumes. Evelyn's Diary.
A beautiful Pepys' Diary. The Spectator, 8 volumes
edition of the
Spectator. (a beautiful edition, Little, Brown & Com-
pany). Southey's Wesley, Nelson, and The
Doctor, 3 volumes. Machiavelli's Prince.
Plutarch's Lives, 4 volumes. Plutarch's
Morals, 4 volumes. Meditations of the
Emperor Marcus Aurelius Antoninus (Lon-
don, 1708). La Bruyère's Characters (London, 1702). Erasmus's Praise of Folly,
and Colloquies, 2 volumes (London, 1711.
These authors should be read in old edi-
Blowing the tions. It is like blowing dust off vellum).
dust off vel-
lum. Coleridge's Table Talk. Sir Thomas More's
Utopia. (How the figments of his imagination have been realized in the later life
of the race! Original thinking seems like
commonplace.) Scott's Old Mortality,
Ivanhoe, and Guy Mannering. (These
three embody the magician's genius, and
save space and money.) Bulwer's My
Novel. Reynard the Fox. Lover's Le-
The story gends and Stories of Ireland (to get the
of Barny
O'Reirdon. story of Barny O'Reirdon). Joubert's

Thoughts. Parton's Voltaire, 2 volumes. Manzoni's Betrothed Lovers. John Woolman's Journal. Paul and Virginia ("the swan-song of old dying France"). Alger's Oriental Poetry. Sterne's Works, 4 volumes. Mandeville's Fable of the Bees, 2 volumes. (A work that is destined, as Swift would say, to "go down the gutter of time," for its boldness and originality, notwithstanding its burning by the Middlesex grand jury.) And lastly (deserving to be mentioned amongst the first) Xenophon's Memorabilia of Socrates. In all, something like 220 volumes. As to cost, I once saw a rich Californian pay as much for sets of Irving and Cooper in tree calf as would have bought the whole collection, including a respectable case to put it in. My friend the doctor wears a stone in his shirt-front, which makes him ridiculous with sensible people, and excites the cupidity of every ruffian that meets him, that would buy the whole precious collection twice over. I believe I shall call it My Grindstone Library. What mind would not be sharpened by consulting it? And where, pray, would one begin to weed? I think I shall have an artisan inscribe the significant name at the top, just under the

The last, but one of the best.

"My Grindstone Library."

moulding.   **It is not** likely that many applications will be made to borrow from it.

A Quaker of the Wool- man type. **One of** my best **friends is an** old-time Quaker, of the John Woolman type, which is rapidly disappearing.   He is an excellent man, and a call from him always refreshes me.   He carries an atmosphere of peace and good-will with him.   **He** is an honest **man.   He is** what he seems to be, and seems to be what he is.   **No** wonder that such men, under the leadership of George *George Fox.* **Fox, should** have disturbed the **complacency of** conformists in England.   Macaulay describes the tempest of derision the sturdy shoemaker **raised** by declaring that it was a violation **of** Christian sincerity to designate **a** single person by a plural pronoun, and that it was an idolatrous homage to Janus and Woden to talk about January and Wednesday.   Teufelsdröckh, in Sartor, pronounces the most remarkable incident **in** modern history, not **the** Diet of Worms, still less the battle of Austerlitz, Waterloo, **Peterloo,** or any other battle, but George *Making to himself a suit of leather.* **Fox's making to himself** a suit of leather. " Sitting **in his stall ;** working on tanned hides, amid **pincers,** paste-horns, rosin, swine-bristles, and **a** nameless flood of rub-

bish, this man had nevertheless a living
spirit belonging to him." It is very evident
that Macaulay had anything but a warm *Macaulay.*
side for the sect that by its zeal and direct-
ness and courage had done so much toward
turning all that had been considered established upside down. Southey, too, never let
an opportunity pass without hitting the rev-
olutionary peace sect a blow. And Coleridge — how merciless! — as exhibited in a
passage in his Table Talk. He is speaking
of modern Quakerism, be it remembered
— unlike the original type, exemplified by
my worthy and amiable friend. " Modern *Coleridge*
Quakerism," he says, " is like one of those *quoted.*
gigantic trees which are seen in the forests
of North America — apparently flourishing,
and preserving all its greatest stretch and
spread of branches ; but when you cut
through an enormously thick and gnarled
bark, you find the whole inside hollow and
rotten. Modern Quakerism, like such a
tree, stands upright by help of its inveter-
ate bark alone. Bark a Quaker, and he is
a poor creature." One of the most distinguished ministers of the Society of Friends
in America at an early day thought it *Very curi-*
necessary, when speaking in his Journal of *ous.*
a morning walk outside Geneva (where he

was tarrying in the interest of his society),
to apologize for taking a look at Geneva
Lake and the mountains. " I walked," he
says, "out of the city (Geneva) and viewed
Asceticism. the Alps and the lake ; this I did for the
sake of the walk." The peculiar style of
the sect — more in vogue a few years ago
than now — is shown in the letter — pronounced to be authentic : "Friend John : I
desire thee to be so kind as to go to one of
those sinful men in the flesh called an attorney, and let him take out an instrument,
with a seal fixed thereto ; by means where-
" The out- of we may seize the outward tabernacle of
ward taber-
nacle." George Green, and bring him before the
lambskin men at Westminster, and teach
him to do as he would be done by : and
so I rest thy friend in the light.   M. G."
Their sermons, too, were sometimes very
peculiar and concise, though their meetings
were apt to be silent.   On one occasion,
when a large audience was assembled, the
only words spoken were by a lady — very
A short ser- deliberately : "Help yourselves, and your
mon.
friends will like you the better."   I have
heard my mother say that she once went
several miles, on horseback with her two
boys, to a Quaker meeting in the woods,
and that the remarkable sermon preached at

the time (by a lady too) had made such an
impression upon her that she could never
forget it.   It also was delivered in a very
measured, deliberate manner, and did not
disturb in the least the stillness, serenity,
and solemnity of the meeting : " Beware of *Another still shorter.*
puffèdupness !" Its brevity and conciseness
made it memorable ; and my mother often
repeated it with effect when her half-dozen
self-conceited boys were most intolerable.
The early hostility of the sect to music
was a part of their religion, and was very
decided.   When Jenny Lind appeared in a *Jenny Lind.*
Western city in 1851, and a limited number
of the society in a neighboring town had
announced their intention of hearing the
" Nightingale," the conscientious "head of
the meeting " "felt a concern" to arise in
fourth day (Wednesday) meeting and admonish his hearers that there was a "foreign girl named Jane Lynde trapesing up
and down the land whose voice was said to
provoke the birds to sing, and he would warn *Provoking the birds to*
especially the young of the meeting to be- *sing.*
ware the wiles of all such worldly persons."
One John M., a Friend of like strictness,
was shocked to learn that his son-in-law,
Jonathan T., who kept a country store in a
village some miles away, was selling musical

instruments. The venerable good man, after a night of prayers and tears, determined to visit his son-in-law, and break up the sinful traffic. Arriving in front of his son-in-law's store, he called him into the street — refusing peremptorily to go in, till the object of his visit was accomplished. "Jonathan!" sternly spake John, "I hear thee keeps musical instruments for sale; does thee?" "A few; but"— The zealous John — interrupting — demanded that they be produced at once, to be destroyed — promising to refund whatever they had cost. They were accordingly brought out, and in the presence of the interested crowd in the street—with the manner of a prophet of Israel destroying the images of Baal — he proceeded violently to tear out their tongues. They were jews-harps!

Breaking up a sinful traffic.

With the manner of a prophet of Israel.

It is recorded that some one at a dinner-table in England remarked that Landseer must have been once a dog himself, as he could see his resemblance to one; remarking at the same time upon the distinguished painter's arrogant manner, love of contradiction, and despotic judgment. I have myself remarked the resemblance referred to in some of the portraits of the great

Landseer's resemblance to a dog.

man ; and thought how natural that he
should have painted his canine friends so
perfectly. Charles Darwin's resemblance *Darwin's*
likeness to a
to a monkey is certainly very marked : one *monkey.*
engraving I have seen of him makes him
the very image of a well-known species of
ape. His long and peculiar investigations
may have had the effect to develop the
likeness in him, latent perhaps in us all.
For three generations we know that the
Darwins were engaged in much the same
line of study. Erasmus, the grandfather of
Charles, must have been deep in " species "
questions, for he had inscribed upon a seal
which he used the significant words, "om-
nia ex conchis " — all from oysters. Per- *"All from*
oysters."
haps there never existed a more honest
investigator than Charles Darwin, and it
is impossible to estimate the effect of his
investigations upon society and thought.
The new civilization of Japan seems to a
great extent to have accepted his conclusions and teachings, along with those of
kindred contemporary scientists and philosophers ; and it is said that many of the
most enlightened of that strange people
are interested in them above everything
else — even above Christianity itself.
Whatever men may think of Darwin's

facts and philosophy, they must admire his
industry, his enthusiasm, and, above all,
his candor.   He even went so far as to
make a list of thirty-four authors and
works in which he finds his theory of evo-
lution more or less distinctly foreshadowed.
As to his conclusions, always so guardedly
expressed, what close observer has not
time and again been led to suspect the possible truth of them?   Once I took an intelligent monkey by the hand (extended to
me at the request of the keeper), and looking him in the face, I found it impossible
to repress a certain feeling of brotherhood.
Its little palm felt like the shriveled hand
of an infant, and its eyes had a look of
comprehension and affinity.   I shall never
forget the sensation that came over me on
the occasion.   Important events, a hundred
of them, have occurred to me since that
time, and been forgotten, but that leave-
taking with the poor performing man-ani-
mal is as fresh as any event of yesterday.
Hawthorne, after observing a sick monkey
in the Zoölogical Gardens in London, went
home and wrote in his note-book, " In a
future state of being, I think it will be one
of my inquiries, in reference to the mysteries of the present state, why monkeys

*A remark-
able instance
of candor.*

*A feeling of
brotherhood.*

*Hawthorne
in his note-
book.*

were made. The Creator could not surely have meant to ridicule his own work. It might rather be fancied that Satan had perpetrated monkeys, with a malicious purpose of parodying the masterpiece of creation." Swift must have been struck *Swift in Gulliver.* in some such way, or we should not have had the remarkable passage in Gulliver, relating to the conduct of the gigantic monkey in Brobdingnag — as big as an elephant — which seized the famous traveler in his bed-room, and carried him to the top of an out-house, sixty feet high, where the monster was seen by hundreds in the court, sitting upon the ridge of the building, holding Gulliver like a baby in one of *Gulliver in one of the monkey's fore-paws.* his fore-paws, and feeding him with the other, by cramming into his mouth some victuals he had squeezed out of the bag on one side of his chaps, and patting him when he would not eat. Wilkie Collins must have been impressed with the apparent close relationship existing between man and monkey or he could never have had his hero, Count Fosco (a great creation), *Count Fosco* do as he did with the organ-grinder in the story. Fosco stopped at a pastry-cook's, went in (probably to give an order), and came out immediately with a tart in his hand. An Italian was grinding an organ before the shop, and a miserable little shriveled monkey was sitting on the instrument. The count stopped, bit a piece for himself out of the tart, and gravely *The count's* handed the rest to the monkey. "My *preference.* poor little man!" he said, with grotesque tenderness, "you look hungry. In the sacred name of humanity, I offer you some lunch!" The organ-grinder piteously put in his claim to a penny from the benevolent stranger. The count shrugged his shoulders contemptuously, and passed on. When Frederick the Great made short excursions he was in the habit of carrying *Voltaire.* Voltaire with him. In one of these Voltaire was alone in a post-chaise which followed the king's carriage. A young page, whom Voltaire had some days previous caused to be severely scolded, resolved to have revenge; accordingly, when he went before to cause the horses to be prepared, he told all the postmasters and postillions *The king's* that the king had an old monkey, of which *monkey.* he was so fond, that he delighted in dressing him up like a person belonging to the court, and that he always made this animal accompany him in his little excursions; that the monkey cared for no one but the king, and was extremely mischievous ; and that, therefore, if he attempted to get out of the chaise, they were to prevent him. After receiving this notice, all the ser- *How the servants abused him.* vants of the different post-houses, when- ever Voltaire attempted to get out of the carriage, opposed his exit, and when he thrust out his hand to open the carriage-door, he always received two or three sharp blows with a stick upon it, accompanied with shouts of laughter. Voltaire, who did not understand a word of German, could not demand the least explanation of these *No explanation.* singular proceedings ; his fury became extreme, but it only served to redouble the gayety of the postmasters ; and a large crowd constantly assembled in consequence of the page's report, to see the king's monkey, and to hoot him. Throughout the journey, things passed off in this fashion ; but what completed the anger and vexation of Voltaire was, that the king thought the trick so pleasant, that he refused to punish the inventor of it. This story is set down in Madame de Genlis' *Monkeys as food.* Memoirs. Monkeys form an article of food throughout tropical America, and the difference between feeding upon them and man-eating, to the susceptible traveler, is not very apparent. The meat is tough, and keeps longer than any other in that climate. They boil it with unripe papaws to make it tender. The Indians told Gibbon that "the tail is the most delicate part when the hair is properly singed." In Japan, monkey meat is prepared in a chafing-dish with onions and sweet sauce. A traveler in that country says he found it tender, but almost tasteless. At one inn he saw the freshly severed head of a very large monkey hung to the chain supporting an iron pot for cooking. It was ghastly, grim, and pallid, painfully human in color and expression, and the dead face seemed to change in the rising smoke. He had no desire to taste monkey after that. Instances of imitativeness in monkeys are sometimes curiously suggestive of humanity. In the following instance the consequences were disastrous. It is a story of a monkey brought home by a sailor to his wife. The animal got to be a household pet, and was always about the kitchen when the woman was at work. The yard was full of chickens, and every now and then they would come into the room to pick up crumbs. Whenever they became too much of a nuisance, the good woman

The tail the most delicate part.

Painfully human.

A household pet.

would throw a few grains of powder in the fire to frighten them out with the flash. One day the sailor's wife was away, and the monkey undertook to manage the kitchen. He watched the chickens very *His conduct.* carefully, and when the kitchen was pretty well filled with them, he took down the powder-horn and threw it all in the fire, blowing himself and everything sky high. I once saw a swinging monkey in a zoölogical garden who seemed to consider and estimate the angles and distances with as much apparent accuracy and skill as the *Skill of a* greatest expert in a gymnasium. He never *swinging monkey.* missed his purpose a single time, and his aims were as varied as they were interesting. Lord Sandwich trained up a huge baboon that he was fond of to play the part of a clergyman, dressed in canonicals, and make some buffoon imitation of saying grace. One of the species of baboon called the mandrill, was well known in London some years ago. He was called "Happy *Happy* Jerry." He was excessively fond of gin *Jerry.* and water, and of tobacco. An ape, one of the gibbons, produces an exact octave of musical sounds : ascending and descending the scale by half-notes, so that this monkey "alone of brute mammals may be said to sing." Various kinds of monkeys make laughing or tittering sounds when pleased.

When much enraged. The face of one species at least, when much enraged, grows red. Mr. Sutton carefully observed for Darwin a young orang and chimpanzee, and he found that both always closed their eyes in sneezing and coughing. Keepers of monkeys in zoölogical gardens say that a common disease with them is softening of the brain. Many of the peculiar diseases of the females are the same as in the human species of the same sex.

A minute tail. A writer in Nature says that in the human skeleton a minute tail is to be seen, though none is visible in the unmutilated adult body. In the earliest stages of our existence, however, there is for a short time a real tail of considerable relative extent, but in the development of the body it becomes stationary, so as rapidly to become altogether overshadowed and hidden. "Many years ago (says Darwin) in the Zoological Gardens, I placed a looking-glass

Two young orangs. on the floor before two young orangs, who, as far as it was known, had never before seen one. At first they gazed at their own images, with the most steady surprise, and often changed their point of view. They then approached close, and protruded

their lips towards the image, as if to kiss
it, in exactly the same manner as they
had previously done towards each other,
when first placed, a few days before, in
the same room. They next made all sorts *All sorts of grimaces.*
of grimaces, and put themselves in various
attitudes before the mirror; they pressed
and rubbed the surface; they placed their
hands at different distances behind it; and
finally seemed almost frightened, started
a little, became cross, and refused to look
any longer." When Dr. Duchesne gave to
a monkey some new article of food, it ele- *Elevated its eyebrows.*
vated its eyebrows a little, thus assuming
an appearance of close attention. It then
took the food in its fingers, and, with low-
ered or rectilinear eyebrows, scratched,
smelt, and examined it, — an expression
of reflection being thus exhibited. Sometimes it would throw back its head a little,
and again with suddenly raised eyebrows
reëxamine and finally taste the food. But
more remarkable than all is the seeming
consciousness of evil, and apparent instinct *Instinct of Satan.*
of Satan, that these very human animals,
under certain circumstances, seem to ex-
hibit. Turtles and serpents are sometimes
put into the cells of the poor captives.
They do not much care for the turtles, but
the snakes are the very devil.

As I walked up and down my library
to-day, stopping occasionally to turn over
musingly some old well-worn volumes, I
could not help wondering if the time spent
Certain so-called sciences. upon certain so-called sciences was not
about all lost. Like every other young
man of studious habits, I thought I must
know the mind, and so I read metaphysics.
I read Locke, until my brain was weary,
trying to comprehend his theory of "in-
Depressed. nate ideas." I was depressed, — feeling
acutely that my failure to comprehend him
was on account of my own mental inability. I read Dugald Stewart; and though
delighted with his didactic eloquence, I did
not understand his system as I thought I
should. I read Sir William Hamilton : the
result was the same. I was discouraged
— especially with my own estimate of myself. Sometimes I lamented that I had
read these books at all ; but never could
tell why, till, years after, I met with the
Judgment of Carlyle. judgment of Thomas Carlyle, which perfectly rested my uneasy mind. " This
study of metaphysics, I say, had only the
result, after bringing me rapidly through
different phases of opinion, at last to de-
No right be-ginning or ending. liver me altogether out of metaphysics. I
found it altogether a frothy system, no

right beginning to it, no right ending. I
began with Hume and Diderot, and as
long as I was with them I ran at atheism,
at blackness, at materialism of all kinds.
If I read Kant I arrived at precisely op- *Kant.*
posite conclusions, that all the world was
spirit, namely, that there was nothing material at all anywhere ; and the result was
what I have stated, that I resolved for my
part on having nothing more to do with
metaphysics at all." I thought, too, with
all other studious boys and young men,
that I must become acquainted with what
Archbishop Whately called "catallactics, *Catallac-*
or the science of exchanges" (political *tics.*
economy). I read Smith, and Malthus,
and Ricardo, and others; and as I pro-
gressed the less I knew, or the more I
became lost in the endless complication of
conflicting calculations and theories. All
the time vaguely suspecting — not having
the courage or ability to conclude, with De
Quincey — that "nothing could be postu-
lated, nothing demonstrated, for anarchy *Nothing de-*
as to first principles was predominant." *monstra'ed.*
And I was never quite at ease with my-
self on the subject till I encountered Dan- *Webster's*
iel Webster's dictum as to the so-called *dictum*
science, very clearly expressed in a letter

to a friend : " For my part," says the
great lawyer, and statesman, and profound
thinker, " though I like the investigation
of particular questions, I give up what is
called the science of political economy.

*Not a sci-
ence.*

There is no such science. There are no
rules on these subjects so fixed and in-
variable that their aggregate constitutes
a science. I believe I have recently run
over twenty volumes, from Adam Smith
to Professor Dew ; and from the whole, if
I were to pick out with one hand all mere
truisms, and with the other all the doubtful propositions, little would be left."

*Lord, have
mercy.*

Lord, have mercy upon me, a miserable
sinner. In my wretched physical and
moral state, I like to think upon the possible good man, as I find him outlined in
George Herbert, Goldsmith, and others, to
say nothing of the New Testament. I like
to think of that pleasant Sunday morning, when I heard the good Episcopalian,
Dr. Muhlenberg, preach a sermon in Dr.
Adams's Presbyterian church, in behalf of a

*Christian
charity.*

Lutheran mission. The theme was Christian charity. And the spirit of the Teacher
was in every word. Once or twice he lost
his place from (it appeared to me) pure ex-

altation of feeling — being lifted up out of himself into a higher medium. Rapt, transported, for the moment, his countenance showed him to be. The heaven of his hopes, and the heaven of the hopes of all, he was in a sense already enjoying. The smile of the Lord was the feast of his soul. The difficulty of finding his place again, seemed only to be the difficulty of readjustment. The good man ! And many and many good men there are, though not so conspicuous. The bigot's calculation, that nine hundred and ninety-nine of every thousand souls are predestined to be lost, is not the calculation of the possessor of a human heart which knows itself, or feels at all a tithe of the irremediable that lies about it. A right-minded man has some consciousness of human weakness and of the difficulty of the human lot — neither of which existent verities should for a moment be lost sight of while considering any system of philosophy, government, or religion especially. Religion is for men, as government and philosophy are ; and as men cannot violently be made over, they must be taken as they exist. Any system must fail that requires the impossible. A true Christian Church has been defined to be an associa-

The heaven of all.

The bigot's calculation.

Religion.

Theology.

tion of men for the cultivation of knowledge, the practice of piety, and the promo-
tion of virtue. The temple of theology is
ever crumbling. Extremes and nice dis-
tinctions in faith are being more and more
forgotten or subordinated ; and while a
common basis is being discovered, it is felt
to be wise by the sects to " press differences tenderly. Religion is too essential
to cling to any dogma." It is the amalgam

*Christian-
ity.*

of Christianity that is destined to fuse the
churches. The elements are slowly prepar-
ing, to be inevitably compounded. There
are encouraging signs. A recent traveler
in Europe speaks of visiting an immense
brown church in Heidelberg, with imposing
steeple, and statues in the niches on the
walls, which he supposed to be a Catholic
cathedral. On entering he observed that
it was divided in two parts by a wall in the
centre, and discovered that one end of the
church was Catholic, and the other end
Lutheran, both worshiping under one roof.

Imagine it!

Imagine an American village of five thousand souls, with a dozen or more sects of
Christians, all worshiping together in one
temple. How soon the different sects would
become ashamed of their petty differences,
and what a power such a compound organ-

ization would become. It would soon be
an influence from the centre to the ends of
the earth. As it is, the different sects —
all claiming a common purpose — find it
impossible to hold a few meetings together
without bickering. How the devil laughs *The devil laughs.*
at all such proceedings, and rejoices at
every new device to divide his enemies.
Whenever in any religious faith, dark or
bright (says a recent writer), we allow our
minds to dwell upon the points in which
we differ from other people, we are wrong,
and in the devil's power. This is the es-
sence of the Pharisee's thanksgiving — *The Phari-see's thanks-giving.*
" Lord, I thank thee that I am not as other
men are." At every moment of our lives
we should be trying to find out, not in what
we differ with other people, but in what we
agree with them ; and the moment we can
agree as to anything that should be done,
kind or good (and who but fools could n't ?)
then do it ; push at it together ; you can't
quarrel in a side-by-side push ; but the moment that even the best men stop pushing,
and begin talking, they mistake their pug- *Pugnacity mistaken for piety.*
nacity for piety, and it 's all over. Chris-
tianity, said Warburton to Spence, seems
to have received more hurt from its friends
than its enemies. By their making things

part of it, which are not so; or talking of things as very material to it, which are very little so. The sects discuss one an-

Moral whet-stones. other somewhat as they use whetstones, Coleridge said, to sharpen their moral discrimination and consciences. But the battle-cries of Sobieski and Ibrahim are not for this day. All the world knows with Swift, that you may force men, by interest or punishment, to say or swear they believe, and to act as if they believed: you can go no further. Beliefs, therefore, are less and less regarded, in comparison with Christianity itself. Men, it has been said,

Special be-liefs. may be tattooed with their special beliefs like so many South-Sea Islanders; but a real human heart with Divine love in it, beats with the same glow under all the patterns of all earth's thousand tribes. "'T is not the dying for a faith that 's so hard, Master Harry," said the trooper [Dick Steele], "'t is the living up to it that is difficult." Ah! what mighty intellects have been employed in the world to divide it, in matters of religious faith, and what multitudes of lives have been sacrificed to keep

Gloomy the-ologies. it divided! When the gloomy and awful theologies become curiosities, how prodigious will the intellects of their inventors

appear! Robert Hall pronounced Jonathan Edwards the greatest of the sons of
men. "That he was a man of extraordinary endowments (remarks Dr. Holmes,
in his defense of the doctors against the
clergy) and of deep spiritual nature, was not
questioned, nor that he was a most acute
reasoner who could unfold a proposition
into its consequences as patiently, as con-
vincingly, as a palæontologist extorts its
confession from a fossil fragment. But it
was maintained that so many dehumaniz-
ing ideas were mixed up with his concep-
tions of man, and so many diabolizing at- *Diabolizing attributes.*
tributes embodied in his imagination of
the Deity, that his system of beliefs was
tainted throughout by them, and that the
fact of his being so remarkable a logician
recoiled on the premises which pointed his
inexorable syllogisms to such revolting
conclusions. When he presents us a God,
in whose sight children, with certain not
too frequent exceptions, 'are young vipers,
and are infinitely more hateful than vipers'; when he gives the most frightful
detailed description of infinite and endless *Endless tor-*
tortures which it drives men and women *tures.*
mad to think of, prepared for 'the bulk of
mankind'; when he cruelly pictures a fu-

ture in which parents are to sing hallelu-
jahs of praise as they see their children
driven into the furnace, where they are to
lie 'roasting' forever, — we have a right to
say that the man who held such beliefs and
indulged in such imaginations and expres-
A burden.   sions, is a burden and not a support in reference to the creed with which his name is
associated.   What heathenism has ever approached the horrors of this conception of
human destiny?   It is not an abuse of language to apply to such a system of beliefs
Christian
pessimism.   the name of Christian pessimism."   It has
been said that if the Christian apostles, St.
Peter and St. Paul, could return to Rome
they might perchance inquire the name
of the Deity who is worshiped with such
mysterious rites in its magnificent temple:
at Oxford or Geneva they would experience
less surprise ; but it might still be incum-
bent on them to peruse the catechism of
the church, and to study the orthodox com-
mentators on their own writings and the
Words of
the Master.   words of their Master.   It certainly would
appear to them that the sects had departed
far away from the teachings and example
of the Founder, and that love to God and
love for man were in danger of being buried
forever under the rubbish of dogmas and

symbols. At the same time it would appear very evident to them that materialism
was speciously deified, and that mammon in
all its forms was exalted, if not worshiped.
It was only the other day that I happened
to be looking out of the window, and wit- *A signifi-*
cant scene.
nessed, at the corner of the street opposite,
the meeting of a priest and a poor working-
man of his church. The uncovered head
of the poor man immediately and obeisantly
went down in reverence — half-way to the
pavement; while the priest made no movement, nor gave the slightest sign of recognition. The priest and the one rich man *The priest*
and the rich
of his congregation next met, an instant *man.*
after, near the same spot. The scene was
significantly changed. The rich man in
this instance gave no sign of recognition
that could be perceived ; the priest it was
— the recognized priest of the Most High
— that bowed down abjectly to Mammon.

No man ever existed, I suppose, who did
not regret the acquaintance and association
of certain persons, on account of their particular bad influence over him. The evils
that men suffer and inflict are so often directly traceable to the influence and exam- *Evil com-*
munications
ple of evil communications, that reflective

persons find it difficult to separate them. One remarkable man it was my ill-fortune to know intimately for a time in my early life, of whom I am constantly reminded in all my evil thoughts and short-comings. His unusual ability and nature made him a very dangerous acquaintance. There was so much subtile penetration in his disparaging observation, and so much genius in his malice, that he was fascinating perforce. For forty years I have been trying to rid myself of the effects of a few months' association with him, and for forty years regretting that I ever met him. The considerable distinction he afterwards attained did not much modify his character; so that I have often been astonished that he died in his bed a natural death — that somebody didn't kill him, or that he didn't kill himself. I have wondered, too, that, as he was always secreting venom, he did not die of an excess of it. In Brazil, an opinion prevails that whoever has been bitten by a boa-constrictor has nothing to fear from any other reptile. Adapting the language of Sydney Smith applied to O'Connell — What a happy condition that of the man who had suffered abuse from my venomous acquaintance. It did not enter into

Genius in malice.

Often astonished.

the head of Goethe that the publication of
Werther would be followed by an epidemic
of suicide.   It would have surprised Dick- *Suicide.*
ens to learn that a copy of Martin Chuzzlewit, open at the chapter describing the
suicide of Jonas Chuzzlewit, was found by
the side of a man who committed suicide
in New York.   Evil influence, like the
"damned spot," will not "out."   In a corner of the Black Museum in London hang
the clothes of a clergyman who murdered
his wife some years ago.   So carefully had
the murderer washed his trousers and his
coat-sleeves, that the blood-stains could *Blood-stains.*
only be discerned with difficulty at the
time of the investigation.   But since the
coat and trousers have been hanging on
the Black Museum's walls, the stains have
come out close and thick.   "We many
times notice that here," the visitor is told.
It deserves to be noticed (says Hawthorne,
in his English Note-Books) that some small
figures of Indian Thugs, represented as en- *Indian*
gaged in their profession and handiwork   *Thugs.*
of cajoling and strangling travelers, have
been removed from the place which they
formerly occupied in the part of the Brit-
ish Museum shown to the general public.
They are now in the more private room,

and the reason of their withdrawal is, that, according to the chaplain of Newgate, the practice of garroting was suggested to the English thieves by this representation of Indian Thugs. Said James T. Fields in a lecture on Fiction in Brooklyn, " I re- *The Pom-* cently paid a visit to the Pomeroy boy, *eroy boy.* who was sentenced to be hanged for killing three children, but whose sentence was afterward commuted to imprisonment for life. I asked him if he read much. He said that he did. 'What kind of books do you read?' said I. 'Mostly one kind,' he *Dime novels.* said — 'mostly dime novels.' 'What is the best book you have read?' I asked. 'Well, I liked Buffalo Bill best,' he replied. 'It was full of murders, and pictures about murders.' 'Well,' I asked, 'how did you feel after reading such a book?' 'Oh,' said he, 'I felt as if I wanted to do the same.'" Another remarkable instance of the direct influence of bad literature upon boys, I remember to have seen referred to authentically in a Western newspaper. *Murdered* The bodies of three murdered women were *women.* discovered in a house in a village. They were considerably decomposed — lime hav- ing been sprinkled over them ; and dime novels of the most objectionable character were found in the room, which had to all appearance been read by the murderer after the murders had been committed. The suspected murderer was a son of one of the murdered women, and committed suicide soon after the crime was discovered. It was proven, at least, that he had borrowed the novels. He was but eighteen years old.

The boy-murderer.

Sin and bile, in the judgment of the excellent Hannah More, are the two bad things in this world. As to the unmitigated badness of the latter, my sufferings for the last few days fully attest. My whole system is inundated by it, and my complexion is a miserable yellow. My doctor talks wisely about it, but does not relieve me. My mind, too, is affected by it, and I find it very difficult indeed to think clearly or healthfully. Ah! exclaimed an intellectual giant — suffering as I suffer from this distressing malady — what a dismal, debasing, and confusing element is that of a sick body on the human soul or thinking part! But for the counteracting influence of my good books, I know not what I should do. On the front of the first national library founded in Egypt was en-

Sin and bile.

A sick body a confusing element.

graved, "The medicine of the mind." The body, however, is often a despot, and the thinking part is in such subserviency that it can only very feebly exert itself. In all countries, says Leigh Hunt, the devil (to speak after the received theory of good and ill) seems to provide for a due dimi-

Health and happiness dependent upon diet. nution of health and happiness by something in the way of meat and drink. The northern nations exasperate their bile with beer, the southern with oil, and all with butter and pastry. I would swear that Dante was a great eater of "fries." Poor

Buttered toast. Lord Castlereagh had had his buttered toast served up for breakfast the day he killed himself. The opinion of a book, it has often been remarked, depends very much on the state of the liver. It has even been suggested that some charitable reformer may have been sagacious enough to discover a way to fuse sects and harmonize Christians, but that the liver of the book-taster consigned the desideratum,

The responsibility of printers. above every other, to oblivion. The responsibility of printers! A very eminent physician firmly believed that he had more than once changed the moral character of a boy by leeches to the inside of the nose. On the other hand, the mind affects the

body as directly, and sometimes very curiously. George Eliot wrote to one of her
friends, "If you were to feel my bump of
acquisitiveness, I dare say you would find
it in a state of inflammation, like the ' veneration ' of that clergyman to whom the
phrenologist said, ' Sir, you have recently *Religion and science.*
been engaged in prayer.'" Jean Paul ob-
served that the stomach of the butterfly
shrinks up when his wings are spread. Sin
and bile! Bile and sin! It has been said,
by a profound student of human nature,
that when an elevated mind looks into the
abyss of evil beyond a certain depth, it is *The abyss of evil.*
seized with a vertigo, and can no longer
distinguish anything. In the Crystal Palace, Hawthorne saw nothing in the sculp-
tural way, either modern or antique, that
impressed him so much as a statue of a
nude mother by a French artist. In a sitting posture, with one knee over the other,
she was clasping her highest knee with
both hands ; and in the hollow cradle thus
formed by her arms lay two sweet little *Two sweet little babies.*
babies, as snug and close to her heart as if
they had not yet been born, — two little
love blossoms, — and the mother encir-
cling and pervading them with love. But
an infinite pathos and strange terror were

given to this beautiful group by some faint
bas-reliefs on the pedestal, indicating that
the happy mother was Eve, and Cain and
Abel the two innocent babes. Cain and
Abel! Abel and Cain! Alas! There is,
says a writer upon mental disease, a destiny made for a man by his ancestors; and
no one can elude, were he able to attempt
it, the tyranny of his organization. The
power of hereditary influence in determin-
ing an individual's nature, which, when
plainly stated, must needs appear a tru-
ism, has been more or less distinctly recognized in all ages. Solomon proclaimed it
to be the special merit of a good man that
he leaves an inheritance to his children's
children; on the other hand it has been
declared that the sins of the father shall be
visited upon the children unto the third
and fourth generations. It was a proverb
in Israel that when the fathers have eaten
sour grapes the children's teeth are set on
edge; and it was deemed no marvel that
those whose fathers had stoned the prophets should reject Him who was sent unto
them — "Ye are the children of those who
stoned the prophets." Complaint having
been made to Caligula that his daughter,
two years old, scratched the little children

*Cain and
Abel.*

*Solomon's
proclama-
tion.*

*Caligula's
daughter.*

who were her play-fellows, and even tried
to tear out their eyes, he replied, with a
laugh, " I see ; she is my daughter." Ri-
bot speaks of a native New Zealander, intelligent and curious, connected with the
chief families of his country, who accompanied an English traveler to London for
education, but owing to the imperfect de- *Education
vs. heredity*
velopment of his mind he could understand nothing of European civilization, and
interpreted everything according to the
notions of a savage. Thus, when a rich
man passed, he would say, " That man has
a good deal to eat," unable to understand
wealth in any other way. The missionary
societies sometimes adopt Chinese infants *Chinese infants.*
and have them educated in European insti-
tutions at great expense ; they go back to
their own country with the resolve to prop-
agate the Christian religion, but scarcely
have they disembarked when the spirit of
their race seizes upon them ; they forget
their promises, and lose all their Christian
beliefs. It might be supposed that they
had never left China. The fact itself (says
Mill, in his great little book On Liberty),
of causing the existence of a human being, *Responsibility of caus-
ing the ex-
istence of a
human be-
ing.*
is one of the most responsible actions in
the range of human life. To undertake

this responsibility — to bestow a life which may be either a curse or a blessing — unless the being on whom it is to be bestowed will have at least the ordinary chances of a desirable existence, is a crime against that being. Especially, another has re-

Transmitted defects.

marked, no one who transmits defects of his or her own, whether physical or moral, can help feeling that he has wronged the child in handing them down to it. The compunction must be particularly painful when the defect is moral. When a father in his son, or a mother in her daughter,

Perversities outcropping.

sees weaknesses and perversities outcropping which they clearly recognize as old personal property, they must doubt whether they are the persons who should punish the young offenders ; and it is not difficult to fancy that children, by some dim kind of instinct, partially discover the injustice of being scolded for teeth set on edge by the very people who have eaten the sour

Grievous indeed.

grapes. It seemed grievous indeed to Charlotte Brontë that those who have not sinned should suffer so largely.

I have been thinking how very remarkable is the thoroughly enlightened, cultivated man of this age of the world: he is

a marvel. Open and receptive to every
suggestion and influence, every thing has
taught him, as every thing is constantly
teaching him. Intelligence is in the air,
and flies on the wings of the wind. It is
not possible for him to avoid breathing
and absorbing it. There is a character in
Dickens, or somewhere in fiction, whose
occupation was in the wine-cellar amongst
the butts and pipes ; he never drank anything, but he was always comfortable by
absorption. So it is at this day with an
open, healthy nature ; it has but to open
its eyes and ears and pores (so to speak)
to be enlightened. What we call study is
not so necessary to intelligence as once.
Every thing is an object-lesson, and teaches
irresistibly. The results of genius and
skill are everywhere, and they have been
so intelligently worked out that they tell
the processes of development. Machines
are so much like the men they compete
with and so often eclipse that they communicate. Printed pages are to be had for
the picking up. Science opens its doors
gratuitously. Art everywhere adorns and
instructs. A good brain coöperating with
a good heart, with all opportunities and
facilities at every turn, must develop good

A marvel.

A character in Dickens.

Study not as necessary as once.

Art adorns and instructs.

character and sovereign enlightenment.
The possible man, of full growth, under
such encouraging and stimulating circumstances, is pleasant to contemplate. On an
island in the sea, one bright Sunday morning, not many years ago, I met a good
representative specimen of high manhood,
which sometimes appears to my memory,
filling it full, to the exclusion of everything
beside. It was after breakfast that I had
sauntered down to my favorite rock, where
I delighted to lounge when the weather
was favorable. It sloped gently to the
west, and was sheltered from the morning
sun by the ledge behind. It overlooked a
diminutive bay (the size of this library
room), which was always particularly interesting to me at low tide. At such times
the kelp lay exposed, and specimens of
star-fish and sea-urchins were sometimes
visible. The puff of the locomotive was
seen but not heard ten miles away, on
the mainland. In favorable atmospheres I
thought I could discern Mt. Washington,
defining itself as a cloud in the distance.
It was an interesting spot to dream at, as
it is an interesting spot to dream of. I
found my rock occupied, by a gentleman
in gray — say of fifty years of age ; but

A good rep-
resentative
specimen.

A favorite
rock.

The diminu-
tive bay.

A gentleman
in gray.

there was room enough for two, he insisted, and moved over. I had never seen
him before ; but his manner and atmosphere of gentility and good-breeding were
assuring, and I sat down. Something was
said of the morning, or the tide, or a pass-
ing sail. The little bay, that he had just *The little bay inter- ested him.*
discovered, seemed as interesting to him
as it was to me. Its situation and accesso-
ries were referred to in a compendious sentence or two, that denoted his full comprehension of them. His observations upon
the rock formations visible, showed him *Rock forma- tions.*
familiar with the theories and conclusions
of geology. His reference to a sea-urchin
had the observation and intelligence of a
naturalist in it. He called particular attention to a long serpentine line of kelp, and *Kelp.*
in a few sentences gave me an amount
of information of the remarkable sea-weed
that I have never wholly forgotten. How
it grows in lower latitudes on every rock
from low water mark to a great depth, both
on the outer coast and within the chan-
nels ; how every rock near the surface is
buoyed by this floating weed, — thus af-
fording good service to vessels navigating *Of service to sailors.*
near the stormy land, and saving many a
one from being wrecked. Three hundred

and sixty feet is the length it had been known to attain. He compared the great aquatic forests of the southern hemisphere with the terrestrial ones in the intertropical regions, and said that if in any country a forest was destroyed, he believed not nearly so many species of animals would *Effects of its destruction.* perish as in the former, from the destruction of the kelp. Amidst the leaves of this plant numerous species of fish live, which nowhere else could find food or shelter ; with their destruction the many cor- *Creatures that would perish.* morants and other fishing-birds, the otters, seals, and porpoises, would soon perish also ; and the Fuegian savage, the miserable lord of that miserable land, would redouble his cannibal feast, decrease in numbers, and perhaps cease to exist. From considering the remarkable plant of the sea, and discoursing upon it, he naturally passed, in contrast, to the ship of the desert. Alive or dead, his information was, *The camel.* that almost every part of the camel is serviceable to man : her milk is plentiful and nutritious ; the young and tender flesh has the taste of veal ; a valuable salt is extracted from the urine ; dung supplies the deficiency of fuel ; and the long hair, which falls each year and is renewed, is coarsely manufactured into the garments, the furniture, and the tents of the Bedouins. It struck him, as it strikes the traveler, as something extremely romantic and mysterious, the noiseless step of the camel, from *His noiseless step.* the spongy nature of his foot ; whatever be the substance of the ground — sand, or rock, or turf, or loose stones — you hear no footfall ; you see an immense animal approaching you, stilly as a cloud floating on air ; and, unless he wears a bell, your sense of hearing, acute as it may be, will give you no intimation of his presence. The Arabs, he said, could live five days without victuals, and subsist for three weeks on nothing else but the blood of their camels, who *His blood.* could lose so much of it as would suffice for that time, without being exhausted. Thence the interesting man passed in the same intelligent way to the populations of the East — to the effects of commerce and Western ideas upon China and Japan ; to the opening of Africa, the wonderful discoveries there, and their probable influence upon European trade and emigration. Thence to the adaptation of governments *Adaptation of governments.* to the new growth of nations. How all the religions were perceptibly changing in a similar manner. Noting, as he passed, some of the effects of the rushing progression upon the habits and dispositions of men — increased restlessness, growing materialism, and apparent diminution of faith being of the few results suggestively referred to. His acute and comprehensive view — his easy passage from one remote part of the world to another — reminded me of a sermon I had lately heard preached by Dr. Hitchcock — certainly one of the most vigorous pulpit thinkers in the world — in which the whole round earth was made to appear apart to the hearer's eye ; he turned it about as a teacher turns his revolving globe, and pointed to spots here and there, dimly or conspicuously lighted by Christianity and Christian civilization — all with so much freedom, simplicity, and intelligence, that it hardly occurred to me to guess, much less to conceive the prodigious diligence and exhausting study that had been necessary to the presentation of the subject so comprehensively, so easily, and so naturally. This many-sided, cosmopolitan man, on my rock, talked of finance, but not of the machinery of the banker's office ; of commerce, but not of lines of railway or steamships ; of government, but not of office-holders or of office-

Acute and comprehensive.

The whole round earth to the eye.

A cosmopolitan man.

holding ; of polity, not politics ; of religion, not churches. I could not have guessed, at the end of his conversation, in what part of the world he lived ; with what political party, if any, he acted ; with what denomination he worshiped ; in what occupation he had made his money. He had asked no questions, nor anticipated any. In all that he had said, there was no show of vanity, bigotry, intolerance, dogmatism, or aggressiveness. He had talked and I had listened. There was that in his manner which said, It happens so ; next time a reverse ; you will talk and I will listen. The bell at the hotel called us to a late dinner. At the table, a glass of wine was brought to me by a servant from another part of the dining-hall, with the name and compliments of my companion of the morning. I returned my own name, of course, with the usual acknowledgment. After dinner he came to me as if he had known me always, extending his hand, and calling me by name — saying, that he wished to present me to his wife. With the accomplished lady I walked up and down the piazza for a few minutes, when my acquaintance (it seemed to me for ages in another state of being) made his appearance again, regret-

He asked no questions, nor anticipated any.

A glass of wine.

His wife.

ting to take leave, as they were to embark
in an hour for New York, to sail thence by
Wednesday's steamer for Europe. I have
never seen or heard of the remarkable man

The impres-
sion of him
distinctly in
memory.
since; yet he made such an impression
upon me, and I remember him so distinctly,
that I cannot help setting him down as
a specimen of the thoroughly enlightened
and cultivated man referred to in the beginning.

The business
of reform-
ing.
The business of reforming — re-forming
— making over — how interesting! An
occupation for saints, philosophers, and
heroes. The instinct to unmake and re-
make is very prevalent, and develops early.
Only now and then a man is found who is
not a born reformer. Himself perfect, the
reformer would have everybody like himself. If a hundred persons were stopped
at haphazard in the streets of Paris, says
Dumont, and a proposal were made to
them to take charge of the Government,

Ninety-nine
of one hun-
dred.
ninety-nine would accept it. Mirabeau accepted the post of reporter to the com-
mittee on mines without having the slightest tincture of knowledge on the subject.
Men enter upon politics like the gentleman who, on being asked if he knew how

to play the harpsichord, replied, "I cannot
tell, I never tried, but I will see." Socrates
used to say, that although no man under-
takes a trade he has not learned, even the
meanest, yet every one thinks himself suffi- *Every man*
ciently qualified for the hardest of all trades, *a governor.*
that of government.   As I have said, the
instinct to govern — re-form — unmake —
re-make — re-create — develops very early.
A boy only thirteen years old, who had
been reading newspapers of one party till
he became impressed with the belief that
the opposite party was in every way and in
every thing essentially and totally corrupt,
asked his mother, impatiently and indig-
nantly, "Why don't the Government abol- *A boy's ques-*
ish the Democrats?"   His question was *tion.*
radical, and in the spirit of the reformer.
A little legislation, in his estimation, was all
that was necessary.   Bolingbroke, though,
understood such matters very differently.
"It is a very easy thing to divine good
laws ; the difficulty is to make them effective.   The great mistake is that of looking *The great*
upon men as virtuous, or thinking that they *mistake.*
can be made so by laws."   "Publish few
edicts," said Don Quixote to Governor
Sancho Panza, "but let them be good ; and,
above all, see that they are well observed ;

for edicts that are not kept are the same as not made, and seem only to show that the prince, though he had wisdom and authority to make them, had not the courage to insist upon their execution. Laws that threaten, and are not enforced, become *King Log's experience.* like King Log, whose croaking subjects first feared, then despised him." Canon Wilberforce, in a sermon in York Minster, speaking of the impossibility of restraining men's appetites and passions, said, "This is not the platform ; and yet, before this altar, I declare that there is nothing at which the devils laugh more than at an act of parliament." "Man," said Douglas Jerrold, "will not be made temperate or virtuous by the strong hand of the law, but by the teaching and influence of moral power. *Acts of parliament.* A man is no more made sober by act of parliament than a woman is made chaste." There is a speech by the blunt Duke du Sully to an assembly of popish ladies, who were railing very bitterly at Henry the Fourth, at his accession to the French *The Duke du Sully to some popish ladies.* throne ; "Ladies," said he, "you have a very good king, if you knew when you are well. However, set your hearts at rest, for he is not a man to be scolded or - scratched out of his kingdom." "The idea of reform," says Judge Brackenridge, in Modern Chivalry, "delights the imagination. Hence, reformers are prone to reform too much. There is a blue and a better blue ; but in making the better blue, a small error in the proportion, of the drug, or alkali, will turn it black." Leigh Hunt, when a very young man, wrote a comedy which was never acted or published. It was entitled A Hundred a Year, and turned upon a hater of the country, who, upon having an annuity to that amount given him, on condition of his never going out of London, becomes a hater of the town. "I cannot, for my part," says an acute essayist, "understand how the frame of mind which is eager for proselytes should survive very early youth. I would not conceal my own views, but neither could I feel anxious to thrust them upon others ; and that, for the very simple reason that conversion appears to me to be an absurdity. You cannot change a man's thoughts about things as you can change the books in his library. The mind is not a box, which can have opinions inserted and extracted at pleasure. No belief is good for anything which is not part of an organic growth and the natural product of

Reformers prone to reform too much.

The contrary effect.

The mind is not a box.

a man's mental development under the various conditions in which he is placed. To promote his intellectual activity, to encourage him to think, and to put him in the way of thinking rightly, is a plain duty; but to try to insert ready-made opinions into his mind by dint of authority is to contradict the fundamental principles of free inquiry." "Attempt to shape the world according to its poetry," said Dr. Riccabocca, "and you fit yourself for a mad-house. The farther off the age is from the realization of their projects, the more the philosophers have indulged them. Thus, it was amidst the saddest corruptions of court manners that it became the fashion in Paris to sit for one's picture, with a crook in one's hand as Alexis or Daphne. Just as liberty was fast dying out of Greece, and the successors of Alexander were founding their monarchies, and Rome was growing up to crush in its iron grasp all states save its own, Plato withdraws his eyes from the world, to open them in his dreamy Atlantis. Just in the grimmest period of English history, with the axe hanging over his head, Sir Thomas More gives us his Utopia." The error of Jeremy Bentham and of John Locke, it has been remarked,

Ready-made opinions not to be inserted.

A fashion in Paris.

Sir Thomas More, with the axe over his head.

was in supposing that they in their closets could frame de novo a code for the people. The latter prepared a code more than a century ago for one of the North American colonies, which proved a signal failure. Burke, upon being conducted by Erskine to his garden, through a tunnel under the road that divided the house from the shrubbery, all the beauty of Kenwood (Lord Mansfield's place) and the distant prospect suddenly burst upon them. "Oh," said Burke, "this is just the place for a reformer — all the beauties are beyond your reach." "Sun! how I hate thy beams!" exclaimed the sick philosopher; but the sick philosopher could not tear the sun out of the sky. This old world has been several thousand ages a part of the universe, and she cannot be easily jostled out of her place. The race of man has been as long developing; and to go back to the beginning to begin the work of working it over — re-forming it — re-creating it — would discourage any but courageous reformers of the aggressive type, who, in their zeal and sublime confidence, think all things possible of accomplishment. At the beginning they must begin, to be thorough. The evil — accumulating for thousands of ages -- must be

Burke's exclamation.

Discouraging to any but courageous reformers.

radically eliminated, to make room for the good that was lost at the Fall. Hobhouse saw it differently. He once said to Hunt that " the only real thing in life was to be always doing wrong, and always to be for-given for it." Commenting upon the re-mark, the poet asks, " Is not that pretty and Christian?" Whoever would transform a character, it has been well said, must undo a life history. The fixed and un-changing laws by which events come to pass hold sway in the domain of mind as in every other domain of nature. As things are, it is not always easy to know what is right or best. Movement is not always progress. Parry, in his Polar expedition, while urging northward along the ice his sleighs and Samoyede dogs, found, when the sun, bursting through the fog, revealed his position, that he had been unconsciously traveling several degrees to the southward, since he had been journeying on a mass of floating ice borne by the ocean currents to the south. The devil — the principle of evil — whatever you call him or it — all men agree in regarding the arch-enemy. Resist him until resistance becomes habit, and he will not much trouble you; permit him liberties, and you are his, body and

Pretty and Christian.

Movement not always progress.

The arch-enemy.

spirit. King Zohak, as Southey relates it, gave the devil leave to kiss his shoulders. Instantly, two serpents sprang out, who, in the fury of hunger, attacked his head, and attempted to get at his brain. Zohak pulled them away, and tore them with his nails. But he found that they were insep- arable parts of himself, and that what he was lacerating was his own flesh. *Parts of himself.*

Alas! Alas! I am troubled now with my eyes. Fortunately, with all my varied and multiplied diseases and ailments, my eyesight has remained unimpaired, until within a very few days. My doctor is not quite clear as to the trouble, and suggests that I should consult a specialist. The thought of blindness terrifies me. To sit in darkness the remainder of my days, without the resource of vision to fortify me against innumerable distresses, would be awful. Without my usual supply of honey from my library I should starve. My faculties must be generously fed, and the food they require is of the richest and daintiest varieties. "My mind my king- dom is." As I sit in my easy-chair, how- ever rheumatism may rack me, my eye can run along the shelves, and my mind enjoy *Troubled with his eyes.* *Honey from his library.*

the society of a century of worthies of all the ages. With the companionship of the gods, the gout, even, may be endured.

The gods sympathize.

The gods sympathize. They all have known suffering, and derision, and isolation. "To live alone is the chastisement of whoever will raise himself too high." Tortured, imprisoned, beheaded, many of them were. "Awful is the duel between man and the age in which he lives!" Starved often, they fed on ambrosia, and are immortal.

Jacob and Daniel

Jacob, with the heavens for a tent, and the stones for a pillow, saw the angels ascending and descending. Daniel, declining the king's wine and meat, and living on vegetables and water, interpreted the king's vision. Generous memory must supply me for a while. My doctor says I must not read: that a little reading, even, is perilous. And writing — the least — he absolutely prohibits. This record of my idleness, therefore, must be laid aside. Sorry; for this essaying at composition is more nearly an amusement than anything that I attempt. In a limited way I shall

A cherished scheme.

be driven to adopt a scheme that has long been in my mind. I long have thought that if I were a rich man I should have a dozen competent persons, or more, to read for me. They should be selected for their special fitness, and paid generous salaries, that their minds might be entirely at ease, and wholly at my service. The world abounds in scholars, who would be glad of such employment. Books would be supplied to them liberally. Twenty thousand dollars a year I should enjoy expending in that way. I should then feel that I might be fairly acquainted with the moral, intellectual, and material progress of the whole earth. Certain of the sciences I should have men employed upon of the highest order that could be obtained. Certain parts of the world I should have explored and studied to the utmost extent that books would permit. Eleemosynary and missionary efforts of every description I should have known and tabulated. The great growth of the Great West — known to geographers only a few years ago as the Great American Desert — I should have noted as intelligently as swift progress would allow. I should have a man for South America and the Pacific Islands, who should report to me every sign of growth and civilization in those isolated regions. I should have another for Africa, who should be specially competent for that

Scholars to read for him.

Of the highest order.

The Great West.

South America.

most interesting field. The rivers and

The Dark Continent. the lakes of the Dark Continent he should explore with Livingstone and Stanley, and others, and carefully **set down** every new settlement, with **its resources** and purposes, as far as could **be** ascertained. India should be invaded and ransacked by **a**

China. competent reader. And China, with all her peculiarities, philosophies, and superstitions, should be carefully and searchingly studied. China! — that strange country, where "objects terrestrial and celestial, objects visible and invisible, and objects real and imaginary, are made the recipients

A strange fact. of homage; but among them all there is **not one the object of** the worship of which **is to** make the devotee more pure and more sincere, more honest, more virtuous, or more holy. The object whose attainment is desired is always selfish, sensual, or

Japan. secular." And Japan — a more wonderful country still — I should keep a man, or two **men, constantly** engaged in investigating. **If** practicable, a thoroughly intelligent person **who had** traveled in that country **should be** employed. The decaying religion **of the Japanese** he should be instructed to comprehend **if possible**; and especially he should be instructed to observe whatever

is taking its place. The awful poverty of *Awful poverty.*
that old country where humanity is such a
drug, and where the graveyards are greater
in population than the towns ; yet Dai-
koku, the god of wealth, is in every house
and worshiped by every inhabitant, with
body and spirit ; — where the children are
taught the gloomiest fatalism from the ear- *The gloomiest fatalism.*
liest moment of comprehension ; — where
soap is not used, — only a little sand in a
running stream ; — where the children do
not cry ; — where the process of milking a
cow is unknown ; — where such necessary
articles as pins are never seen. A traveler
in the interior of the country for hundreds
and hundreds of miles never heard a child *No child cried.*
cry ! " Such queer crowds," she says ; " so
silent and gaping, remaining motionless for
hours, the wide awake babies, on the mothers' backs and in the fathers' arms, never
crying."   " In Yusowa," she writes, " I
took my lunch in a yard, and the people *A scene.*
crowded in hundreds to the gate, and those
behind being unable to see me, got ladders
and climbed on the adjacent roofs, where
they remained till one of the roofs gave
way with a loud crash, and precipitated
about fifty men, women, and children into
the room below, which fortunately was va-

Scant cos-
tumes.
cant. Nobody screamed!" The scant cos·
tumes of a large proportion of the population in the interior are curious. The same
traveler **reports** that **the** younger children
wear nothing at all but a string and an am·
ulet. "Could anything," she asks, **"be a**
A strange
sight.
stranger sight than a decent-looking, mid-
dle-aged man, lying on his chest in the
veranda, raised on his elbows, and intently
reading a book, clothed only in a pair of
spectacles?" Many of the men in the
A hat and a
fan.
rice-fields wear only a hat, with a fan at-
tached to a girdle. **As the** lady **rode**
through Yokote, a town of ten thousand
souls, the people rushed out from the baths
to see her, men and women alike, without
Art.
a particle of clothing. **Art, too, I** should
have **a competent** reader in — an artist if
possible — to report the achievements of
the greatest painters and sculptors. The
Literature.
novel fields of literature should be scoured;
in a word, every thing knowable, present
and past, should **be** known, as far as was
practicable, and communicated to me, at
stated hours, to suit my convenience —
intelligently, enthusiastically, exuberantly.
$20,000 a
year.
Twenty thousand dollars a year expended
in that delightful way, for enlightenment,
entertainment, **and** occupation, **I** should
consider cheap and magnificent pleasure.

"The burden and the mystery of all this unintelligible world." "Through mystery to mystery." There is nothing beautiful, sweet, or grand in life, it has been said, but in its mysteries. The sentiments which agitate us most strongly are enveloped in obscurity : modesty, virtuous love, sincere friendship, have all their secrets, with which the world must not be made acquainted. Hearts which love understand each other by a word ; half of each is at all times open to the other. Innocence itself is but a holy ignorance, and the most ineffable of mysteries. Infancy is only happy because it as yet knows nothing ; age miserable because it has nothing more to learn. Happily for it, when the mysteries of life are ending, those of immortality commence. Heraclitus, it is known, composed a book On Nature, which he deposited in the temple of Diana. The style in which it was written was purposely obscure, that it might be read only by the learned, he being afraid, if it were to afford entertainment to the people generally, that it would soon become so common as to procure him only contempt. This book, says Lucretius, gained extraordinary reputation, because nobody understood it. Da-

Through mystery to mystery.

Innocence a holy ignorance.

Heraclitus's book.

Nobody understood it.

rius, king of Persia, having heard of it, **wrote** to the author to induce him to come and explain it to him, offering him, at the same time, a handsome reward and a lodging in his **own** palace ; **but** Heraclitus re- *Swift.* fused to go. Swift's profound knowledge of human nature led him to envelop his publications in all the mystery possible. After the Tale of a Tub and Battle of the Books had been handed about in manuscript for years, they **were** published anon- *Voltaire.* ymously. Voltaire's latest French editors give a list of his one hundred and eight pseudonyms. The mystery and obscurity of The Divine Comedy gave it the interest and almost the importance of a new religion for a century or more. Steele **says the art of** managing mankind is only to make them stare a little to keep up their astonishment ; to let nothing be familiar to them, but ever to have something in their sleeve, in which they must *Rabelais.* think you are deeper than you are. Rabelais struck terrible blows, then hid himself in his **humor. His** general incomprehensibleness was his strength with the **multitude, which laughed** without always knowing what it was laughing about — the **object satirized being** presented in all sorts of disguises. The wisdom and beauty of Tristram Shandy : how few readers discover or appreciate them, compared with the greater number who delight in its nonsense and coarseness. The influence and fame of the Letters of Junius were more the *Junius* result of the mystery of their authorship than of their essential ability. The fact that they have been attributed to so many is evidence that many were thought capable of producing them. While books continue to be printed upon the subject of their origin, and the wisest of men exercise themselves in speculating upon the same, copies of the famous Letters will multiply, *The famous* and be thought necessary to every library, *Letters.* though the events which produced them have long ceased to be of much interest, except to the most curious student. What were romance - writing without mystery ? The story-writer must not only be ingenious in inventing his mysteries, but he must be skillful in carrying them, to succeed with the public. Great is the mys- *The mystery* tery of godliness. In the attempt to know *of godliness* the unknowable, creeds have been produced and sects organized. If its teachers had taught the practice of Christianity continually, and not expended themselves in developing systems of theology, all Christendom would long ago have been a united army against Satan. Quiet is thought to be proof of reserved force. The individual who keeps his own counsel is always overestimated by the public. The same is the case with the estate of a man who is careful to be out of debt. The lady who does not cheapen herself by careless association and much display, is invested and clothed by the public with every virtue. All the world acknowledges that felicitous reserve which La Rochefoucauld has called "the mystery of the lady." An air of success — how imposing! The world pays court to it unconsciously. Boswell said Beauclerk told a story with that air of the world that had an inexpressibly impressive effect, as if there were something more than was expressed, or than perhaps could be perfectly understood. The influence of what Grammont calls "a compound countenance," is not merely puzzling, it is powerful. Squeers, when introducing Nicholas to his school, looked very profound, as if he had a perfect apprehension of what was inside all the books, and could say every word of their contents by heart if he only chose to take the trouble. Lord

Christendom would have been united.

The mystery of the lady.

A compound countenance.

Thurlow carried himself with such a ma- *Thurlow.*
jestic air that only the more intelligent
ever asked themselves whether any one
could really be as wise as Lord Thurlow always seemed. Talleyrand was a mysteri- *Talleyrand.*
ous character. No one, it appears, could
even intelligently guess his motives or purposes. Suspicion, caution, wickedness,
subtilty, alertness, were natural to him, at
the same time they were so mysteriously
hidden in the recesses of his character,
that their existence as essential parts of
him were hardly thought of. At the very
time he was most ready for a deadly *When ready*
for a deadly
spring, he appeared as quiescent as if all *spring.*
his faculties were dormant. "What does
he mean by it?" he asked, when a celebrated diplomatist fell ill. The report of the
death of George III. having just obtained
circulation throughout Paris, a banker, by
hook or by crook, managed to obtain an
audience with Talleyrand, who was then
Minister for Foreign Affairs. The banker, *The bank-*
er's inter-
who, like many of his financial brethren, *view.*
wished to make a good hit, and thought
the present a favorable opportunity, had
the indiscretion to reveal to the minister
the real object of his visit. Talleyrand
listened to him without moving a muscle

of his phlegmatic visage, and at length replied in a solemn tone, "Some say that
the king of England is dead, others say
that he is not dead; but do you wish to
know my opinion?" "Most anxiously,
prince!" "Well, then, I believe — neither!

Not very satisfactory.

I mention this in confidence to you; but I
rely on your discretion : the slightest im-
prudence on your part would compromise
me most seriously." Madame Flamelin
one day reproached M. de Moutron with
his attachment to Talleyrand. "Good God!
madame," replied M. de Moutron, "who
could help liking him, he is so wicked!"

A compliment.

It was a maxim of his, that a man should
make his début in the world as though he
were about to enter a hostile country ; he
must send out scouts, establish sentinels,
and even be upon the watch himself.
Madame de Staël said of him, "The good
Maurice is not unlike the manikins which
children play with — dolls with heads of
cork and legs of lead ; throw them up
which way you please, they are sure to fall
on their feet." Motley describes the mys-

Philip II.

terious, the jesuitical, the powerful Philip
II. at his writing-table, "scrawling his apos-
tilles." "The fine, innumerable threads
which stretched across the surface of Chris-

tendom, and covered it as with a net, all converged in that silent cheerless cell. France was kept in a state of perpetual *France in perpetual civil war.* civil war; the Netherlands had been converted into a shambles; Ireland was maintained in a state of chronic rebellion; Scotland was torn with internal feuds, regularly organized and paid for by Philip; and its young monarch — 'that lying king of Scots,' as Leicester called him — was kept in a leash ready to be slipped upon England, when his master should give the word; and England herself was palpitating *England palpitating.* with the daily expectation of seeing a disciplined horde of brigands let loose upon her shores; and all this misery, past, present, and future, was wholly due to the existence of that gray-haired letter-writer at his peaceful writing-table." But there was a man in Holland, — more mysterious, more taciturn, more impenetrable, — named William the Silent, — who somehow con- *William the Silent.* trived, every night, while the wily monarch slumbered, to have his writing-desk carefully examined, its contents intelligently noted, and scrupulously reported — the most interesting secret in history. George Washington was a mysterious personage. *Washington.* His nature was impenetrable: it was not comprehended, **and is** not, to this day. No

wonder he was believed to have a charmed
life. Some years after the battle known
as Braddock's Defeat, **an** old Indian sa-
chem visited Washington, **and** told him
that he was one of the warriors in the service of the French, who lay in ambush on
the banks of the Monongahela, and wrought
such havoc in Braddock's army. He declared **that he and his** young men had
singled him out, as **he** made himself conspicuous riding **about the** field of battle
with the general's **orders, and** had fired
at him repeatedly, but without success;
whence they had concluded that he was

under the protection of **the** Great Spirit,
had **a charmed** life, and could not be slain
in battle. The mysterious and the incom-
prehensible **were** readily believed to be
superhuman. An eminent English woman
has remarked it as a singular fact that
whenever **we** find out how anything is
done, our first conclusion seems to be that
God did not do it. The greater the igno-

rance, the greater the power of mystery
over it. Ives, a jailer while Leigh Hunt
was a **prisoner, was a** self-willed, ignorant
creature. **He** was **not** proof, however,
against a Greek copy of Pindar, which he

happened to light upon one day amongst Hunt's books. "Its unintelligible charac- *An unintelligible book.* ter," says the poet, " gave him a notion that he had got somebody to deal with who might really know something which he did not. Perhaps the gilt leaves and red morocco binding had their share in the magic. The upshot was, that he always showed himself anxious to appear well with me, as a clever fellow, treating me with great civility on all occasions but one, when I made him very angry by disappointing him in a money amount. The Pindar was a *The Pindar a mystery.* mystery that staggered him. I remember very well, that giving me a long account one day of something connected with his business, he happened to catch with his eye the shelf that contained it, and whether he saw it or not, abruptly finished by observing, ' But, mister, you knows all these things as well as I do.' " Naturalists refer to the mysterious hypocrisies of nature, and how *The mysterious hypocrisies of nature.* they repeat themselves with more or less completeness and consciousness in the mental life of man. What, it is asked, is the vast force exerted by habit in moulding men into the likeness of the society to which they belong, except a device for making them safe by preventing them from being conspicuous, just as the small green caterpillar is made safe and unconspicuous by its resemblance to the color of the leaves on which it feeds. And is there really any human analogy for the harmless snake and the sphinx caterpillar, which succeed by appearing to possess dangerous qualities which they have not, or more dangerous qualities than any they really have? Hypocrisy is the most specious, the most artful, the most impenetrable, the most mysterious of all the crimes, or sins, or vices. It was only pardonable, one would think, "when theological controversies were converted into engines of oppression, which filled prisons, ruined families, and exiled virtuous men,—rendering hypocrisy one of the necessaries of life." When deliberate and voluntary, it has marvelous advantages. "It is an act," says Molière, "of which the imposture is always respected; and though it may be discovered, no one dares to do anything against it. All the other vices of man are liable to censure, and every one has the liberty of boldly attacking them; but hypocrisy is a privileged vice, which with its hand closes everybody's mouth, and enjoys its repose with sovereign impunity." But how odi-

A suggestive inquiry.

Hypocrisy.

When one of the necessaries of life.

A privileged vice.

ous to God are hypocrites, is denoted in
the force of that dreadful expression, And
his portion shall be with the hypocrites.
"You will find in the Holy Scriptures,"
says Sir Roger L'Estrange, "that God has
given the grace of repentance to persecu-
tors, idolaters, murderers, adulterers, etc.,
but I am mistaken if the whole Bible af- *The Bible affords no*
fords any one instance of a converted *instance of a converted*
hypocrite." *hypocrite.*

Yes; I am a fogy, and not a reformer.
While I cannot help lamenting certain tendencies in our civilization, I do not pretend
to know a way of correcting or diverting
them. Nor am I in any sense a preacher. *In no sense a preacher.*
My physical disabilities and isolation pre-
vent me from being anything but a spectator. I see, and muse, and rarely utter
myself; knowing perfectly well that my
views of many things, when I express them,
are sure to be considered distempered. It
is possible, I admit, that my conclusions *His conclu-sions.*
may sometimes be colored by my dis-
tresses; but what are they in influence,
compared with the active man's prejudices,
jealousies, and interests? If the sick man
be more or less a coward, and only able to
utter feebly his half-truths, the well man *Half-truths*

is ambitious, aggressive, and very much a bully. With his two big fists, and his round veins filled with hot blood, he crushes his way, — as often in defiance of reason as in compliance with it. I here who sit in solitude, deploring, am as apt to be right, possibly, as the lusty partisan or bigot, with his battle-axe of violence. " Reason," says Goethe, " is the property of an elect few." Soundness, equanimity, and true courage, are its legitimate offspring. Few there be that are healthy, in the full sense, and fewer that are wise, and they only at times, under favorable conditions. As anger is madness, so is passion the opposite of reason. At one time, the passionate man is Herculean and inflexible ; at another, he is powerless and plastic. Confucius said, " I have not seen a firm and unbending man." Some one replied, " There is Sin Ch'ang." " Ch'ang," said the Master, "is under the influence of the passions ; how can he be pronounced firm and unbending ? " And this leads me to speak of one of the modern tendencies — in my mind when I began this paragraph. It is, to unman men, — to disindividualize them. Morals therefore, as a result, it seems to me, less and less, are based upon personal

The lusty partisan or bigot.

Passion the opposite of reason.

One of the modern tendencies.

responsibility. Man, in the old-fashioned view, was held a man, — responsible personally for his conduct. His ambition was *The ambition of true manhood.* to breast the current, and to avoid being turned about, as the twig, by every little eddy. If he made the voyage successfully, there was heroism in him. Character was so much effort, and resistance, and endurance. Manliness was held to be accretive *Manliness* and cumulative. Every trial was thought to give another resource, and every conquest to add new power. Each achievement gave increased confidence. Growth was obvious, and calculable, and applicable. To cut the cable, and launch away from conventional helps and restraints, was *The conventionalities.* the common ambition. The individual felt fettered and shorn, if dependent. Before he consented to surrender himself and be subordinate, he must be tried by trusts, perils, and calamities. He aspired to stand an individual man, — responsible to all men *Personal responsibility.* for all the manhood that was in him. Now, the tendency is directly the other way, — to underestimate, if not totally to sink, the individual. The theory is rapidly becoming ascendant that the business of Government is to take care of the citizen. Man is transcended by the machine, and he is

Societies of every sort. disindividualized by societies of every sort. The state educates him ; his social set governs his conduct ; he admits his inability to take care of his earnings, and trusts the savings bank for extremities ; the insurance company provides for his family after his death ; — orders and organizations, *Orders and organizations.* ready-made, of every description, for everything, divine and human, to take charge of his soul, his body, and his estate, here and hereafter.   Instead of boiling up individuals into the species, I would, with Jane *Individuality.* Carlyle, draw a chalk circle round every individuality, and preach to it to keep within that, and preserve and cultivate its identity at the expense of ever so much lost gilt of other people's "isms."   It seems to me as it did to Emerson, that the Deity dressed each soul which he sends into nature in certain virtues and powers not communicable to other men, and sending it to perform one more turn through the circle of *Not transferable.* beings, wrote "Not transferable," and "Good for this trip only," on these garments of the soul.   In the war of civilization upon man, the growth of the individual is systematically discouraged.   Soon he finds himself underestimating himself, in contrast with the omnipotence of organi-

zation and machinery ; then he surren-
ders, and begins living for the day, to be
warmed by the sun, and to be cared for as *Warmed by the sun.*
an incompetent. His efforts cease to be
continuous and persistent. They are not
consciously continued from yesterday, to
be extended throughout to-morrow and to-
morrow, until his work is accomplished
or scheme realized. " The height charms,
the steps to it do not ; with the summit
in view, we walk along the plain." Thor- *Thorough-*
oughness is less and less in vogue. The *ness less and less in vogue.*
world is filling up with Dick Tintos, who
begin to paint without any notion of drawing. Sir Thomas Lawrence's drawings
were so perfect that it seemed a sin to add
any color to them. The same may be said
of Lessing's. Dick was for a time patron- *Patronized for a time.*
ized, as the story goes, by one or two of
those judicious persons who make a virtue
of being singular, and of pitching their own
opinions against those of the world in matters of taste and criticism. But they soon
tired of poor Tinto, and laid him down as a
load, upon the same principle that a spoilt
child throws away its plaything. Misery *Misery took him up.*
took him up, and accompanied him to a
premature grave, to which he was carried
from an obscure lodging, where he had

been dunned by his landlady within doors, and watched by bailiffs without, until death came to his relief.

Another President inaugurated. So another **President has** been peacefully inaugurated (with less than **the** usual measure of nonsense), after all the excitements and threats of a long period of partisan violence. I feel an impulse to expatiate about it all a little ; but my eyes are a perpetual warning. I cannot help, however, *An acute remark.* quoting an extremely acute remark of Harriet Martineau's, in **her** Society in America, published as long ago as 1837 : " Irish emigrants occasionally fight out the battle of the Boyne in the streets of Philadelphia, but native Americans bestow their apprehensions and their wrath upon things future, and their philosophy upon things past. While they do this, it will not be in the power of any President to harm them much or long."

The dimensions of hell. Some nice calculations as to the dimensions of hell are to be found in the old books, and are interesting. Ribera, a curious **divine, calculated** hell **to be** "a material and local fire in the centre of the earth, two hundred Italian miles in diameter." But Lessius, another divine, " would have this local hell far less, one Dutch mile in diameter, all filled with fire and brimstone ; because, as he demonstrated, that space, cubically multiplied, would make a sphere able to hold eight hundred thousand millions of damned bodies (allowing each body six cubic feet), which would abundantly suffice." *Eight hundred thousand millions of damned bodies.*

What a thing is the human brain! Physiologists tell us that a fragment of the gray substance of it, not larger than the head of a small pin, contains parts of many thousands of commingled globes and fibres. Of ganglion globules alone, according to the estimate of Meynert, there cannot be less than six hundred millions in the convolutions of a human brain. They are indeed in such infinite numbers that possibly only a small portion of the globules provided are ever turned to account in even the most energetic brains. " What else than a natural and mighty palimpsest is the human brain?" exclaims De Quincey. " Everlasting layers of ideas, images, feelings, fall upon it as softly as light. Each succession seems to bury all that went before. And yet, in reality, not one *The human brain.* *Six hundred millions of globules.* *A mighty palimpsest.*

is extinguished." Coleridge tells a story of a servant maid, who, in a fever, spoke Greek, Hebrew, and Latin ; Erasmus mentions an Italian who spoke German, though he had forgotten that language for twenty years ; there is also a case recorded of a butcher's boy who, when insane, recited passages from the Phèdre which he had heard only once. Every experience a man has, it is asserted, lies dormant within him ; the human soul is like a deep and sombre lake, of which light reveals only the surface ; beneath there lives a whole world of animals and plants, which a storm or an earthquake may suddenly bring to light before the astonished consciousness. A rush of a little alcoholized blood to the brain, the fumes of opium or hasheesh, may produce the most surprising results in the mental machine. A few drops of belladonna or of henbane give rise to fearful visions. A little pus accumulated in the brain, a lesion so slight that the microscope can scarce detect it, gives rise to mental disorganizations called delirium, insanity, monomania. Some years ago, for a change, I spent a few weeks at a country watering place. My condition, at the particular time I am to speak of, was peculiar, — so

Remarkable disclosures.

The human soul like a deep and sombre lake.

The brain a delicate machine.

strange indeed that I believed myself on
the point of a dangerous fever. I had not
consulted a physician, from a lack of confidence in the only one to be had nearer
than the neighboring city. One night, as
I lay in my bed, — the full moon pouring
in its light with such splendor and strength
as to make the smallest objects in the
room visible, — I reflected in terror upon
the risk of passing another hour without
medical advice. My brain was so excited
— the whole mental machinery was running at such a tremendous speed — that it
seemed in the very act of flying to pieces.
The thought of sleep in such a state was
terrifying to me ; to remain awake was
more terrible still. I employed every mental device I could think of to quiet myself,
at the same time I did everything possible
to preserve consciousness. In spite of me,
while contemplating with such composure
as I could the full round moon pouring its
flood of light over me, my eyelids closed,
and I thought I was present early at a
great meeting, assembling in Union Square
to take into consideration the condition of
the Republic, and to devise such means as
might be thought best to aid her in her
distressing extremity. The civil war was

At the point of a dangerous fever.

The mental machinery running at a tremendous speed.

At a great meeting in Union Square.

raging in all its fury. Whole divisions of troops had been cut up, and the tempests

Every interest in peril.
had scattered the fleets. All interests seemed to be in peril, and every citizen was soberly anxious. I had gone to the great meeting early, as I have said. The people were gathering rapidly. They came in carriages, in omnibuses, in horse-cars, on foot. Every vehicle appeared to be crowded, and to leave each one of its passen-

Gathering, gathering.
gers. Soon the people filled the square, and then the broad pavements around the square, and then the broad streets around the broad pavements, and then the broad pavements on the opposite sides of the broad streets, and then the door-steps all round, and windows, and house-tops — a

A hundred thousand.
hundred thousand. I looked under each hat rim and into each hat, and saw every face of every man and woman. I recognized the faces of many familiar acquaintances and the faces of many that I only

Brooding anxiety.
occasionally saw. The same brooding anxiety marked the multitude of visages. The vast assemblage was called to order by Mr. Elliot C. Cowdin, a well-known merchant. His little speech was neat and ap-

A list of vice-presidents.
propriate : I heard each word of it, and every intonation. A long list of vice-pres-

idents was then read — including more than
a hundred **well-known** names — represent-
ing intelligently all interests and all professions of the metropolis. The names
most conspicuous for intelligence, **and**
honor, and wealth, were all there, — not
one, it seemed to me, was omitted. I listened to each one attentively as it was
read out. Now a conspicuous and hon-
ored name in Wall street was pronounced.
Now the name of a flour merchant in
South street. Now a name well known in
importing circles. Now a familiar name in
" the swamp," — the leather region. Jour-
nalism was represented in a few famous
names. The law, and medicine, and science, and architecture, and ship-building,
and the pulpit, were all honorably represented. Of course there was a generous
sprinkling of politicians and office-holders.
I thought, with what prodigious care the
list had been selected, — showing a minute
acquaintance with every interest of the
great town and its best representatives.
Then followed a dozen or more resolutions,
expressing the sense of the people in the
Nation's extremity. They were read with
much intelligence by the secretary, in a
rich full voice, and appeared to be dis-

tinctly **heard** by each **one of the** vast concourse. Every word **seemed to** have been

Expressing a thorough knowledge of the crisis. considered and weighed, — expressing from **first to last a thorough** knowledge and **comprehension of the situation, in** all its **complication** and gravity. **I thought how long the** writer of the resolutions must **have carried** them in his brain and in his **pocket, and how many** enlightened persons **he must have consulted in the course of**

Cut and polished. their preparation. **They were cut and** polished **with the skill of a lapidary.** The **veins of thought were as** conspicuously apparent **as the lines in a precious** stone. **Their scope was broad, and their** observa-

Surprisingly compendious. tion and purpose surprisingly compendious. **Patriotism, experience, and** statesmanship **uttered themselves throughout.** The remarkable resolutions would have filled one **of the broad columns of** The Tribune. **Then Daniel S. Dickinson was** called **on**

A distinguished ex-senator. **for a speech. The distinguished** ex-senator **was at his best. I had never** before seen **his mind in such trim. He seemed** able to **say what he thought, and to** express all **shades and phases of meaning.** There was **logic that went to the marrow** of whatever **he touched, and sarcasm and wit** that en-

His remarkable power. forced it. His remarkable power as an im-

passioned orator never before had struck me
as it did then.   His speech was a long one,
and more than senatorial in breadth and in-   *More than*
cisiveness.   The old flag filled the heavens   *senatorial.*
as Rodman Drake unfurled it there.   The
vast assemblage was electrified.   Then Salmon P. Chase, the secretary of the treas-   *The secre-*
ury, was called out.   Six feet in height,   *tary of the*
he appeared that day to be six feet six in   *treasury.*
his majestic proportions.   He was indeed
statuesque, as he stood for a time, in the
midst of the vast human sea, seemingly un-
impassioned, without uttering a word.   His   *His great*
great two-storied brain seemed teeming   *two-storied*
full of important things to be said.   I had   *brain.*
heard him speak many times, and had lis-
tened to him many an hour in conversation.   Always circumspect in speech before an assembly, he appeared on this
occasion to be unusually and excessively   *Unusually*
deliberate.   His words, every one, had   *deliberate.*
prodigious weight, as they fell, one after
another, from his lips, in solemn cadence.
The knowledge and experience of many
years were close behind every sentence.
The scholar, the jurist, the statesman, —   *The scholar,*
all were embodied in the orator.   His   *the jurist.*
thought was as clear as the mountain air,
his passion was incandescent.   Once or

twice he unconsciously put back his head and gazed, — as I have seen a lion look off apparently thousands of miles into his native jungle, — the sagacious statesman seeming to see, through the smoke of battle and turn of events, the upshot of the mighty struggle. His speech, also, was a long one, — longer by half than any I had ever before heard him deliver. At the conclusion of it the great audience dissolved, and I opened my eyes. I had not changed position in the slightest. The moon was riding the sky through the top of the same pane exactly as when I had seen it last, — filling it full with its overflowing glory. The whole thing, in reality, would have occupied four or five hours, and, reported, would have filled many columns of the daily journal. It is not possible that I could have been unconscious for more than a minute or two. I got up in terror, shut down the windows, and sent off for a heroic physician. What wonder that I express amazement at the human soul, and lose myself trying to conceive the perpetual growth and expansion of the immortal substance, when relieved and emancipated from all earthly entanglements, limitations and miseries ?

The sagacious statesman.

The great audience dissolved.

The remarkable mental operation.

Sends for a physician.

A hopeful interrogation.

My wife — But I have scrupulously re-
frained from gossiping about her in these
hours of my idleness. She herself is too *A tribute to*
wise to keep any sort of personal record. *his wife.*
As was said of the Duchess de Praslin's
murder, "What could a poor fellow do with
a wife who kept a journal **but** murder
her?"

INDEX OF PERSONS REFERRED TO

———◆———

About, 53.
Adams, Dr., 188.
Addison (The Spectator), 170.
Æschylus, 148, 167.
Æsop, 148.
Alexander, 96, 216.
Alger, 171.
Anthon, 165.
Antoninus, Marcus, 148, 170.
Arbuthnot, 140.
Aristotle, 169.
Ashbrook, Lord, 95.
Atterbury, 159.
Austen, Jane, 150, 153, 167.

Bacon, 27, 165.
Ballantyne, Serjeant, 91, 101.
Balzac, 74, 169.
Barbauld, Mrs., 152.
Barnes, 75.
Barrère, 119.
Barrow, 149, 153.
Bayle, 154.
Beaconsfield (Disraeli), 30.
Beattie, Dr., 97.
Beauclerk, 228.
Beckford (Vathek), 169.
Bentham, 216.
Bentley, 151.
Béranger, 152.
Blot, Madame de, 97, 98.
Boerhaave, 73.
Bossuet, 149, 160.
Boswell, 97, 168, 228.
Bourdaloue, 149.
Brackenridge, 215.
Bronté, Charlotte, 150, 167, 204.
Brougham, Lord, 98.
Brown, John, 170.
Browne, Sir Thomas, 83, 149, 153, 168.
Bryant, 166.
Bulwer, 170.
Buncle, John (Amory, Thomas), 81.
Bunyan, 153, 168.

Burke, 217.
Burleigh, Lord, 59.
Burns, 27, 64, 90, 140, 141, 142, 150, 167.
Burton, 149, 168.
Butler, 167.
Byron, 78, 86, 91, 142.
Byron, Lady, 77.

Cæsar, 91, 119.
Calcraft, 91.
Campbell, 73.
Campbell, Dr., 57.
Carlyle, 63, 66, 105, 119, 120, 150, 166, 186.
Carlyle, Jane, 238.
Carlyle, John, 31.
Carnot, 119.
Cary, 30.
Casaubon, 57.
Castlereagh, Lord, 200.
Cervantes (Don Quixote), 70.
Chalmers, 149.
Charles (Charlemagne), 46.
Charles II., 83.
Chase, Salmon P., 247.
Chillingworth, 183.
Cibber, Colley, 97.
Cicero, 64, 148, 160, 168.
Cleopatra, 139.
Coleridge, 29, 75, 88, 134, 150, 170, 173, 192, 242.
Collins, Wilkie, 179.
Columbus, 73.
Confucuis, 108, 169, 236.
Conti, Prince of, 97, 98.
Cooper, 57, 169, 171.
Cooper, Sir Astley, 129.
Cottenham, Lord, 94.
Cowdin, Elliot C., 244.
Cowper, 140.
Crabbe, 74.
Curtis, 166.

Dana, 168.

Dante, 30, 31, 38, 44, 144, 149, 153, 154, 165, 200.
Darius, 225.
Darwin, 168, 177, 184.
De Foe (Robinson Crusoe), 168.
De Quincey, 150, 153, 167, 187, 241.
Dew, Prof., 188.
Dickens, 150, 168, 197, 205.
Dickinson, Daniel S., 246.
Diderot, 187.
Disraeli, Isaac, 149, 168.
Dodsley, 75.
Donne, 153.
Doré, 30, 32, 36, 73.
Drake, Rodman, 247.
Dryden, 89.
Dumont, 212.

Edgeworth, Richard Lovell, 90.
Edwards, Jonathan, 193.
Eldon, 113, 156.
Eliot, George, 201.
Elizabeth, Queen, 85.
Emerson, 26, 55, 107, 150, 166, 238.
Epictetus, 148, 167.
Erasmus, 170, 177, 242.
Erskine, 87, 88, 152, 217.
Esquirol, 24.
Euripides, 153.
Evelyn, 170.

Fabius, 108.
Farr, Dr., 81.
Fénelon, 154, 168.
Fielding, 168.
Fields, 168, 198.
Flamelin, Madame, 230.
Fontenelle, 54.
Foote, 89.
Foster, 136, 137, 139, 149, 167.
Fox, 88.
Fox, George, 172.
Franklin, 59, 87.
Fraser, 93.
Frederick the Great, 180.
Froude, 60, 119, 169.
Fuller, Margaret, 141.
Fuller, Thomas, 169.
Fuseli, 44.

Galen, 163.
Garrow, 87.
Gay, 140.
Genlis, Madame de, 97, 126, 181.
George II., 93.
George III., 229.
George IV., 54.
Gibbon, 162.

Gibbon, Lieut., 182.
Godwin, 167.
Goethe, 26, 103, 153, 158, 168, 197, 236.
Goldsmith, 37, 66, 89, 150, 166, 188.
Grammont, 228.
Gray, 153.
Grey, Countess, 75.
Greeley, 94, 95.

Hahnemann, 15.
Hall, Robert, 149, 193.
Haller, 118.
Hamilton, Sir William, 186.
Hannibal, 95, 96.
Harvey, 118.
Hawthorne, 111, 134, 135, 147, 150, 166, 197, 201.
Hayward, 31.
Hazlitt, 150, 155, 169.
Heine, 36.
Heister, 83.
Henriot, 163.
Henry IV., 214.
Henry, Patrick, 47.
Heraclitus, 225, 226.
Herbert, George, 188.
Herodotus, 136.
Hillard, 168.
Hitchcock, Dr., 210.
Hippocrates, 22.
Hobhouse, 218.
Holmes, 10, 41, 91, 150, 166, 193.
Homer, 31, 148, 153, 165.
Hood, 122.
Holbein, 168.
Houghton, H. O., 166.
Hume, 187.
Hunt, 37, 55, 96, 102, 150, 152, 200, 215, 218, 232, 233.

Ibrahim, 192.
Ingres, 96.
Irving, 30, 167, 171.

Jeffrey, 93.
Jekyll, 70.
Jerrold, 65, 153, 170, 214.
Johnson, 43, 70, 97, 98, 150, 168, 169.
Joubert, 170.

Kant, 187.
Keats, 37, 75, 150.
Kemble, Fanny, 54.
Kempis, Thomas à, 152, 168.
Kinglake, 170.

La Bruyère, 170.
La Rochefoucauld, 167, 228.

Lamb, 27, 70, 75, 88, 123, 134, 167.
Lamartine, 144.
Landor, 100, 168.
Landseer, 176.
Lawrence, 54, 147, 239.
Lay, Benjamin, 59.
Lee, Jack, 144, 145.
Le Sage (Gil Blas), 167.
L'Estrange, 235.
Lessing, 239.
Lessius, 241.
Lever (Charles O'Malley), 168.
Lewis, 169.
Lind, Jenny, 175.
Livius, Titus, 155.
Locke, 186, 216.
Louis XIV., 92.
Lover, 170.
Lowell, 150.
Lucian, 71, 72.
Lucretius, 225.
Luther, 169.

Macaulay, 67, 70, 89, 150, 153, 168, 172, 173.
Macdonald, 65.
Machiavelli, 170.
Mahomet, 34.
Malthus, 187.
Mandeville, 171.
Mansfield, Lord, 217.
Manzoni, 171.
Markham, Miss, 93.
Marlborough, Duchess of, 97.
Martineau, Harriet, 240.
Massillon, 149.
Mathews, 127.
Metastasio, 111.
Meynert, 241.
Mifflin, George H., 166.
Mill, 167, 203.
Milton, 148, 153, 165.
Mirabeau, 212.
Mitchell (Reveries of a Bachelor), 168.
Molière, 234.
Montaigne, 54, 116, 130, 135, 149, 166.
Montagu, Basil, 90.
Montagu, Lady Mary Wortley, 168.
Montesquieu, 58, 86, 130, 170.
Montgaillard, 119.
Moore, 57, 139.
More, Hannah, 199.
More, Sir Thomas, 170, 216.
Morris, Gouverneur, 147.
Motley, 230.
Mountjoy, Lord, 147.
Moutron, de, 230.

Muhlenberg, Dr., 188.
Murray, 31, 93.

Napoleon, 153.
Nasmyth, 90.
Nelson, 170.
Northcote, 169.
Northumberland, Duke of, 117.

O'Connell, 196.
Ossian, 153.
Ovid, 153.

Parry, 218.
Parton, 171.
Pascal, 40, 149, 167.
Patrick, Bishop, 79.
Peterborough, 100.
Petrarch, 144.
Philip II., 230.
Pindar, 232, 233.
Pitt, 88.
Plato, 78, 148, 150, 155, 166.
Pleasonton, 23.
Plutarch, 170.
Pope, 31, 69, 89, 140, 154, 158.
Praslin, Duchess de, 249.
Pyrrhus, 96.

Queensbury, Duchess of, 53.
Queensbury, Duke of, 15.

Rabelais, 11, 149, 169, 226.
Rachel, Mlle., 96.
Ribera, 240.
Ricardo, 187.
Richelieu, 144.
Richter, Jean Paul, 65, 76, 142, 159, 201.
Robespierre, 63, 119.
Robinson, 128, 167.
Rogers, 44.
Roland, Madame, 129, 143.
Rösch, 24.
Ryan, Father, 76.

Saadi, 127.
Saint Pierre (Paul and Virginia), 171.
Sandwich, Lord, 183.
Savage, 169.
Schiller, 149, 153.
Scipio, 95, 96.
Scott, 91, 154, 170.
Seeley (Ecce Homo), 169.
Selden, 108, 169.
Seneca, 166.
Sévigné, Madame de, 168.
Shakespeare, 27, 149, 153.
Shelley, 150.

Sheridan, 142.
Sheridan, Tom, 100.
Smith, Adam, 187, 188.
Smith, James, 157.
Smith, Sydney, 75, 90, 93, 167, 196.
Smollett (Humphry Clinker), 169.
Snooke, Miss Maria, 137.
Sobieski, 192.
Socrates, 148, 171.
South, 149 153.
Southey, 78, 79, 113, 170, 219.
Souvestre, 149, 159, 167.
Spence, 75, 154, 169, 191.
Spenser, 153.
Spinoza, 153.
Staël, Madame de, 230.
Stair, Lord, 92.
Steele, 192, 226.
Sterne, 71, 158, 171.
Stewart, Dugald, 186.
Stowe, Mrs. (Uncle Tom's Cabin), 151, 167.
Suetonius, 148.
Sugden, 94.
Sully, 214.
Swift, 13, 121, 140, 149, 166, 171, 179, 192, 226.

Taine, 102.
Talfourd, 167.
Talleyrand, 104, 229.
Tasso, 144, 170.
Taylor, 130, 153.
Thackeray, 64, 67, 76, 90, 145, 150, 153, 169.
Thomas, General, 107.
Thoms, 89.

Thoreau, 168.
Thurlow, 229.
Ticknor, 168.
Titian, 123.
Tocqueville, 158.
Trollope, 57.

Valerius, 108.
Venable, William H., 78.
Virgil, 31, 46, 153, 165.
Voltaire, 58, 67, 97, 100, 180, 181, 227.

Wallace, 105.
Waller, 50.
Walpole, 53.
Walton, 168.
Warburton, 191.
Washington, 118, 231.
Webster, Daniel, 187.
Webster, Noah, 165.
Wesley, 149, 153, 170.
Whately, 187.
White, 168.
Wilberforce, Canon, 214.
William the Silent, 231.
Williams, Gilly, 63.
Wilson, 167.
Woolman, 171, 172.
Wordsworth, 128, 150.
Wycherley, 48, 49, 50.
Wycherley, Mrs., 49, 50.

Xenophon, 171.

Zenobia, 139.
Zoroaster, 10.
Zschokke, 68.